A CANDLELIGHT ROMANCE

CANDLELIGHT ROMANCES

550 HOME TO THE HIGHLANDS, *Jessica Eliot*
551 DARK LEGACY, *Candace Connell*
552 OMEN FOR LOVE, *Esther Boyd*
553 MAYBE TOMORROW, *Marie Pershing*
556 WHERE SHADOWS LINGER, *Janis Susan May*
557 THE DEMON COUNT, *Anne Stuart*
558 NO TIME FOR LOVE, *Lori Stuart*
559 THE MIDNIGHT EMBRACE, *Barbara Doyle*
560 RUTHANA, *Margaret Nettles Ogan*
561 THE DEMON COUNT'S DAUGHTER, *Anne Stuart*
566 GOLDEN INTERLUDE, *Ellen Searight*
567 RULES OF THE GAME, *Elaine Raco Chase*
568 SPANISH MASQUERADE, *Jane Peart*
569 THE PEACOCK BED, *Joanne Marshall*
574 TENDER IS THE TOUCH, *Anne Shore*
575 ENTWINED DESTINIES, *Rosalind Welles*
576 DARK PARADISE, *Berrie Davis*
577 THE FLOWERS OF DARKNESS, *Elisabeth Barr*
582 JOY RUNS HIGH, *Tilly Armstrong*
583 PRECIOUS PIRATE, *Esther Boyd*
584 TOUCHED BY FIRE, *Mary Lee Stanford*
585 THE WEDDING JOURNEY, *Marjorie Eatock*
590 LOVE IN THE WILDS, *Suzanne Roberts*
591 FORBIDDEN BLESSING, *Lucy Casselman*
592 MORNING ROSE, EVENING SAVAGE, *Amii Lorin*
598 ISLAND LOVESONG, *Louise Bergstrom*
599 EAST TO PARADISE, *Jacqueline Hacsi*
600 DARE TO LOVE, *Candice Arkham*
601 THE MASK OF LOVE, *Katherine Court*
606 COME NOVEMBER, *Virginia Myers*
607 A LOVE TO REMEMBER, *Ida Hills*
608 THE SEARCHING HEART, *Anne Shore*
609 WICKLOW CASTLE, *Mary Hanson*
614 A FLIGHT FOR DREAMERS, *Jane Converse*
615 TO SEIZE THE RAINBOW, *Jo Calloway*
616 LOVE'S SWEET SURRENDER, *Arlene Hale*
617 SHADOWS OF THE HEART, *Lorena McCourtney*
622 COUNTERFEIT HONEYMOON, *Julia Anders*
623 HEART ON HOLIDAY, *Elaine Fowler Palencia*
624 BALI BREEZES, *Esther Boyd*

THE BECKONING HEART

Alyssa Morgan

A CANDLELIGHT ROMANCE

Published by
Dell Publishing Co., Inc.
1 Dag Hammarskjold Plaza
New York, New York 10017

Dell ® TM 681510, Dell Publishing Co., Inc.

ISBN: 0-440-10749-0

Printed in the United States of America

First printing—January 1981

Red sky in the morning
Sailors take warning.
Red sky at night
Sailor's delight
> *Old Sailor's Axiom*

CHAPTER ONE

He looked bleary eyed around the smoke-filled room, then pushed his huge frame from the bar. That damned restlessness was stirring again, the yearning building up that only the tilt of a deck under him would still.

He had had enough of women and the bite of whiskey. He wanted to feel the cool, clean mist of sea spray. He muttered a curse. When were they going to get in touch with him?

Lee frowned as the wind, invited in by the open door, ruffled the chart. She grabbed at the shifting papers. She walked off the distance with the dividers and wrote the total miles under the course line, then looked up resentfully. If the interruptions did not stop, she'd never finish plotting the trip.

"Mr. Williamson is on the dock," she said curtly, not hiding her impatience. The cruise had to be finished that afternoon.

The man took in her tousled blond hair and clear blue eyes, now filled with annoyance.

"I know. Bill sent me here and said he'd follow," he said coolly, reacting to her sharp tone.

She tried to focus on him, nautical figures filling her mind. His thick, well-groomed hair matched dark brown eyes. A black scarf was knotted around his neck, supporting a cast on his left arm.

"Then he'll take care of you." Her relief was evident as she dismissed the tall stranger. She still had to type the itinerary for the trip. The clients would be down tomorrow for one of the chartered sailboats. One of her many jobs was to plot an interesting course on the Chesapeake Bay for those who wanted that service.

She bent over the charting table to check the last leg of the journey against the compass rose, and felt a familiar yearning. She'd give anything to see those places again—Gratitude, Sassafras, Tilghman with the remnants of the skipjacks, and south to the ever-fascinating Smith and Tangier Islands. The names rolled through her mind as a chant—all those lovely places on the Delmarva peninsula, the heavenly coves tucked away in the hundreds of miles of convoluted coastline.

"Have you ever explored the Wye River?" The man was leaning over her shoulder looking at the chart.

"Just the beginning of it," she answered. "I always wanted to make the trip around the island, but the low bridge excluded our sailboat."

"I know," he said, his finger tracing the route. "It's frustrating. There's plenty of water but that ten foot fixed bridge effectively stops the bigger boats."

"We didn't have a decent dinghy or I'd have made my husband take me." She leaned back in her chair, brushing against his bent body. The male smell of pipe tobacco enveloped her, and she closed her eyes in pain.

It had been two years, yet a little thing like that could still trigger a swift reaction. Would she ever be free?

"Is Mr. Porter around?" he asked.

Her eyes flew open in shock.

"I'm sorry," he said in surprise, taking in her blanched face. "Did I say something wrong? Bill told me Lee Porter was here, but I don't see him."

She took a deep breath. Running a hand through her short blond hair, she forced a wan smile.

10

"I'm Lee Porter," she said. "There is no Mr. Porter." He's been gone two long years, her heart thudded.

It was his turn to look startled. "I don't understand. What in the world was Bill talking about?"

The door opened, and Lee's boss walked in. Bill Williamson was a bronzed giant of a man. The sea still breathed from him. A permanent squint from years of peering into long distances didn't hide his piercing blue eyes under bushy brows. His thick white hair was in its usual windblown disarray.

"I see you found her, Craig," he boomed. As always, his presence filled the small office.

"You didn't say Lee Porter was a woman," the man bristled. He was as tall as Bill, and the two glared at each other.

"You said you wanted a good sailor, and I can't recommend any better." Bill's voice was a perpetual shout. "You were looking for someone you could trust, and there's no one better qualified than Lee. I trained her myself," he added with pride. "She's excellent at the helm and as a navigator, and can turn canned food into a gourmet delight."

"But I can't take a woman!" he stormed, his mouth in a tight line.

"Why not?" Bill countered. "You have an aft cabin on your sailboat. You and Biff can sleep there and Lee up for'ard." He dropped his hulk in the ever protesting chair behind his desk.

"You're the one that broke his arm and came for help," Bill pointed out. "I gave you the perfect solution, so what's the beef? Lee is off for the next two weeks, and I know she would drop everything to go sailing."

"Do you two mind telling me what this is all about?" she interrupted. "I'm a little confused. Am I on the market block up for sale?" She frowned at her boss. He was also her friend, her father confessor, her haven in a storm.

"I'm sorry, Mrs. Porter. Bill seems to have forgotten his manners. I'm Craig Lowell." He forced a smile, showing strong, even white teeth.

She looked at him critically, itemizing his rugged good looks. Black brows almost met across a slightly askew nose. His full mouth might be friendly, but not in its present grim line. He was probably in his mid-thirties, she guessed. His dark eyes now snapped with annoyance.

"His son is coming down for two weeks," Bill filled in as Lee nodded at the introduction. "They were planning to cruise in his sailboat. Then he had to break his arm."

"We've been planning this since Christmas," Craig added. "Every letter from Biff has been full of expectations. I hate to let him down."

"Can't your son help you?" she asked. "I've seen some pretty young fellows handle sails remarkably well."

"He's only eight," he explained. "He's enthusiastic but hasn't much experience to help with a forty footer. This was going to fill that gap. Then this had to happen." He looked ruefully at the cast.

"I can imagine how disappointed you both must be," she answered in sympathy.

"So he comes to old Uncle Bill for help," Bill snorted. "I give him the perfect answer and he raises stupid objections because you're a woman. Craig, you'll never find a better sailor. She can pull a mean sail. Between her husband and me, we produced the best first mate to be found on the Bay. I've sailed with her, and I know."

"I can't do it, Bill." Craig's jaw was set, his voice cold and final. "No female."

Lee stiffened to hide her surge of anger. She had mated on several charters. Never once had she been rejected so outright because of her sex. In fact, she was much in demand for the reasons Bill had cited.

Her glance became frigid before she turned her back to return to her task. Some men were insufferable. Male chauvinists.

"I'll have to plan something else. Biff will understand," Craig Lowell continued, unaware of the resentment he had stirred.

"How is the tyke?" Bill's voice went soft as it always did where children were concerned. "Eight, you say? Can't believe it. You have to bring him around. Does he still look like you?"

"So they say." Lee detected the quiet pride in his voice. "He's going to be tall, too. He was all legs the last time I saw him."

The conversation turned to boats, as it always did in the office, and Lee put paper in the typewriter. She had to finish. Tomorrow was Saturday, and the weekend charters would descend to keep them all busy.

The planned cruise was for an old client who had told her what he wanted to see and the time allotted. She had laid out the trip, reviewed it with him, and they would take off confident that she had planned well for them.

Years before, Lee and her husband had spent every free moment hunting out little coves on the big Bay. She now drew on this knowledge to create interesting trips. She had found that most people had favorite places they liked to revisit, but they always wanted one or two surprises. Since her husband's death, she sailed vicariously this way, planning clients' cruises.

When she finished, she found Bill alone, sitting hunched over his desk, frowning over the bills.

"They keep coming in, Lee," he sighed, leaning back in the groaning chair. "At least we're keeping our heads above water. But there must be an easier way to make a living."

She smiled with affection. "Perhaps, but you wouldn't have as much fun."

His eyes crinkled at her. "You're right. I'd dry up away from the sea."

She covered the typewriter. "By the way, who is this Craig Lowell, and where is his son's mother?"

The remnants of her anger still clung. She worked in a primarily man's world but was accepted without reservations. Bill's friends treated her with affection and respect. It rankled her ego to be so summarily dismissed by an arrogant man.

"I captained Craig's father's yacht for nine years until

13

he died," Bill explained. "I watched him grow up and helped make him the sailor he is today.

"He married a very nice girl while in college. Mary died suddenly three years ago. His mother took over with raising the boy as long as she could, but now has a heart condition, I understand. Bill goes to a boarding school now, and camp in summer. It could be a lonely existence for the boy except he knows he is well loved. Craig spends every free minute he can with him. They are very close."

Lee absorbed this information somberly. "What type of work does he do?"

"He's an airline pilot. Flies one of the big jobs."

She raised an eyebrow. "How in the world did he break his arm?"

"Believe it or not, he tripped over a passenger's suitcase," he chuckled. "He's grounded for the duration."

"Well, I hope the male chauvinist finds a mate for his boat," she said wryly. "Sounds like the son might be out of a trip. It will be hard to get someone to crew now. It's still early in the season, and all hands are needed for refurbishing boats. It was a wet spring, and the boat yards are way behind in painting."

"That's what I told him," he grunted.

"It's also an expense to hire a mate," she added.

He snorted. "The Lowells can afford it. They're stinking rich. Craig has a good paying job besides all he's inherited."

Lee closed her desk drawer and stepped outside. The small office looked out at the dock where a dozen assorted sailboats bobbed sleepily from the wake of a distant boat.

Half of the boats were small weekenders, and the others were around thirty feet—fine for one or two couples to cruise for a week or two. The small cove was too shallow for larger boats, but perfect for their small operation.

Sitting on racks were two dozen Sailfish and Hobie Cats. Tomorrow started the weekend and their brightly colored sails would be flitting over the river, the braver ones heading down the Severn River toward Annapolis. It was June week, and the midshipmen and their dates should be out in the Academy boats, a gay sight with all flags flying.

Lee searched the sky. The weather could make or break them. Sun and a gentle breeze would bring customers until all the boats were rented. Those were the times they dreamed of owning a larger inventory. After one or two rainy weekends, however, Bill was happy with the smaller overhead.

There were a few mare's tails high overhead. If those clouds increased, there might be rain by Monday or Tuesday, but by that time of week sailors would be back to work.

She walked past the shed, where Bill did the constant overhauling while she took care of the books and customer service, and arrived at her car.

They had one hired hand. Ron was a college boy with a love affair with the sea. He helped them on busy weekends, and full time through the summer, when any day could be just as rushed as the weekends. They were finding an increased client demand for the evening sail. Exhausted landlubbers in search for relief from the hot, humid weather were eager to catch the evening breezes on the water.

It was a good little business, small but turning a satisfactory profit. She was lucky to have found it in that desperate time two years ago.

The reawakened pain when she had smelled the pipe tobacco, combined with suddenly brushing against a man, re turned. She sat in the car, willing it to go away. Time had helped her heal, but occasionally the pain still caught her unawares, triggered by a half-forgotten memory.

Two years ago the police had come to the door, their unhappy faces telegraphing their news. A rain slick road, a blow out, and Jack Porter and son were no more.

Their old friend, Bill Williamson, managed to reach into the depth of her agony and forced her to come to work for him. His kind face shared her grief, his broad shoulders felt her tears, and his big hands gently molded her back to life.

She sighed as she moved into traffic. On a promising weekend like this she would have been ready for Big Jack to come home from the office. The gear would have been all packed, the ice chest filled, and Little Jack waiting impatiently, jumping with glee. Their pride and joy, he had been a sailor from their first boat trip.

She brushed angrily at the tears. It was behind her, three glorious years to cherish. She had stopped asking why and had climbed out of her numb grief. But the emptiness was still there. Oh, how it was there!

She shook her short blond hair and concentrated on thinking about what she planned to do with her vacation that was to start in two days. She would help with this weekend's rush. Then on Monday she would begin refurbishing her tiny apartment.

The yellow paint sat under the kitchen table. The cheerful curtains and bright new slipcovers were waiting in their boxes. She had had no desire to work on her home the past two years, but this spring when the buds had covered the trees, she, too, had felt a new awakening, a desire to renew herself.

Her world was no longer painted in shades of gray. She saw color and wanted to bring it inside. She was moving out of her suffering, and life again was worth living.

He threw his clothes in the duffel bag. The message had been urgent, as it always was. They didn't give a man time to clear the fumes out of his head or have one last romp.

When a freighter was available, that meant everything was ready, and they moved like clockwork. He knew better than to throw the schedule off. He turned the empty bottle over the glass, hoping for a last drink. A few tan drops dripped out, and he threw it on the floor in disgust.

She moved in the bed, but the noise did not wake her. He looked at the heavy red lips, the full swell under the sheet, and paused.

He hoisted the bag on his shoulder and pulled out his pipe, drawing on its cold stem. He spat the bitter juice on

the floor and went out. Hell, she'd be there when he re-
turned. If not, there'd be others. There always were.

But now he was a captain again, and he went eagerly to
inspect the new ship.

CHAPTER TWO

It was a glorious Saturday, and the people started coming early. Ron had the small boats ready, their colorfully striped sails beckoning. Lee checked out the larger boats for ice, water, and basic supplies. Bill was in charge of the engines and sails.

The customers always seemed to arrive together. Somewhere during the hectic rush she became aware of Craig Lowell standing on the dock, and received a quick introduction to a younger edition of himself.

"Biff, meet Mrs. Porter," he said, then admonished, "Don't get in anyone's way."

Lee smiled and waved to the thin boy. Her first impression was of large brown eyes in a too-thin, sensitive face, and long coltish legs extending from cut-off jeans.

Craig moved swiftly to help Bill untie the lines for an eager party. He moved with surprising agility, keeping his broken arm tucked against his side.

The solemn boy stood forlornly by the piling. "Would you hand me that hose, Biff, so I can fill this tank?" she asked.

He jumped with alacrity, eager to be of assistance. A smile lit his face, making his resemblance to his father even more pronounced.

He became her shadow, manfully struggling with bags

of ice cubes and helping her place them in the ice chests. He watched the hose so the water wouldn't flood when the tanks were being filled. His eyes glowed upon receiving an occasional tip from a customer or a compliment from Lee.

By eleven the last of the large boats were off, and they gathered on the benches outside the office. They were slightly exhausted and refreshed themselves with cans of cold soda.

"I don't know why I think I have to work this hard," Bill boomed, pouring the soda down his throat while Biff stared in awe. "It was a lot easier when I captained for your father, Craig."

"They were good days," Craig admitted. "You and Dad helped mold a small boy to the sea. I fully expected to go to Annapolis and the Navy."

Bill popped another soda. "Instead, you took to the air. What changed your mind?"

Craig frowned as he stared ahead, as if trying to find the answer. "There's very little difference," he said finally with a small shrug. "There is the same feeling of freedom and oneness with the elements. I don't mean the big jobs I'm flying. They're like troop carriers. That's my livelihood. When I'm off duty and not by water, I rent a two seater and do my private thing."

"That's interesting," Lee said in surprise. "I never thought of flying in that way. If I didn't have such an ogre to work for, I'd be sailing forever. There's nothing like the soft slap of water on the hull and the occasional creak of rigging on an easy run. I miss it so!"

Her eyes grew soft with longing. The two men took in her parted lips, wind-tossed blond hair, and straight boyish body in a thin ribbed sweater and faded jeans.

"A hell of a note," Biff growled. "I give her a job and she calls me names."

She grinned affectionately at him, a dimple forming in her left cheek. "You're a slave driver, Bill. Let's face it!"

She looked down at Biff sitting next to her. He was manfully trying to push in the sides of the aluminum can, having noted Bill's habit. His wastebasket was always filled with crushed empty cans.

"Biff was a great help to me, Mr. Lowell," she said, smothering an urge to hug him. He was at an age that would resent any feminine demonstration, yet there was something lonely and forlorn about him. She remembered Bill describing his present life at camps and boarding school. What an empty existence for a young boy!

"He saved me innumerable trips off and on boats as we outfitted them." The thin face turned up to her with a shy smile. "Thank you, Biff. I appreciate all your work."

"I made two dollars and fifty cents," he said proudly, pulling the money out of his pocket to recount the coins.

"With all that money, perhaps you can invite Mrs. Porter to lunch with us," Craig said, rumpling his son's hair with affection. "Can you get away, Bill?"

"No way, but take Lee. I have to help Ron now. We rent the small ones by the hour or half-day, and it keeps us busy."

Lee started to protest. She still felt the sting of yesterday's rejection. He had been unreasonable in rebuffing her services not because of her qualifications, but because she was a woman, and the resentment still burned.

"Will you please have lunch with us, Mrs. Porter?" the boy asked formally. She looked into his wistful brown eyes, and her heart melted.

"It would be my pleasure, Biff. That is if you would have me back in an hour. I have some paper work to finish before I start my vacation Monday."

"It's a promise," Craig said, and she found herself sitting between the two in a sleek black sports car.

"Where to?" Craig asked as he turned into the traffic.

"We're not exactly dressed for anything but shore eating," she said. "There's a place down the street that is very good, and they are used to salty attire. They have steamers that would be just right for me."

"Sounds perfect. Biff and I had planned on getting some this trip. Are their clams good?"

"Sweet and tender if they're like the ones I had last

week." She turned to the boy. "Do you like seafood, Biff? I go on periodic binges."

"I do, but not at school," he said solemnly. "There it tastes like cardboard even when I squeeze a whole lemon over it."

Her heart contracted for the boy. Her son would have been going on four. He would not have had this child's grave demeanor. Little Jack's happy face with its perpetual grin came before her, and she squeezed her eyes shut tight to prevent the unbidden tears from forming.

A huge pot of steamers was placed before them, and they ate with gusto. It was impossible to be formal with clam juice and melted butter dripping from their eager fingers. The mound of empty shells grew as they enjoyed the tender morsels.

"Shall I order another pot?" Craig asked, searching for a stray clam in the bottom.

"I couldn't eat another one," she sighed happily. "Just pour some of that nectar in my cup. I love the broth."

He signaled for clean cups and lined them before him.

"I'll try not to get too much sand from the bottom," he said as he tilted the pot.

"There's nothing wrong with Chesapeake sand." She smiled as she added a dash of celery salt. She leaned back as she put down the empty cup, reluctant to end the pleasant hour. If they hadn't actually buried their animosity, they had hidden it.

"I can face the rest of the day now," she said. "I'll dream of them when I start painting my apartment."

"Is that what you're planning to do with your vacation?" he asked in surprise.

"Yes. Since I won't have the golden opportunity to crew, I can't put off the job any longer." She had to get that dig in. The truce was over.

He had the grace to grimace. "I apologize, Mrs. Porter. I was quite tactless yesterday, but Bill had touted Lee Porter's qualifications so highly, and I was so relieved that my problem was solved, that I felt quite deflated when I found you were a woman, and I was back where I started."

She looked at him quizzically, trying to smother her rising exasperation.

"I'm not selling myself, Mr. Lowell, but why should my being a female turn you off? I've done a lot of crewing for clients, and my sex never came into the picture." She knew her anger was showing and didn't attempt to hide it.

His eyes were mocking as they traveled over her. "If I had the use of my two arms, and didn't have to depend on someone else if an emergency arose, I can imagine having you as a crew would be very interesting and—er—desirable."

Lee fought the blush unsuccessfully at his obvious innuendo and lowered her eyes from his teasing grin.

"As it is, I refuse to harbor the possibility of putting Biff in danger. We both know how storms can whip up suddenly on the Bay, and all hands have to do their job immediately."

"Dad." Biff had been trying to follow the adults' conversation, and a hope was forming in him. "Mrs. Porter sure knows how to handle a boat. She took one out to show some customers how it worked, and she's a whiz at it. You should see how she pulled up the sails and worked the tiller and lines all by herself. Gosh!" He had been impressed as she had maneuvered the weekender back and forth in the small cove in demonstration.

Bill and Craig had also paused in their work as Bill proudly pointed to his protégé.

"Quite a gal, ain't she?" he had beamed as they watched the flawless performance.

Craig looked at his son. "Yes, she did a good job," he admitted. "But there's a vast difference between a twenty-four foot boat and a forty footer."

He signaled for the check, closing the subject firmly.

Seeing his crestfallen face, Lee couldn't resist squeezing Biff's shoulder in comfort while swallowing her own irritation. She still yearned to go sailing. She gave him a friendly wink as they went to the car. He was a polite but sensitive child. Even though his father gave a full measure of love when with him, the times apart must be terribly

22

lonely to him. She had read where pilots on some flights were away from home for several weeks at a time, which would make it necessary for his son to stay at a boarding school.

From his eagerness to help her, she had seen his love for boats, and knew he must be desolate over the abandoned cruise with his father.

Ron called her over when she returned. "I have this young couple who would like to try a sailfish. They've never handled one before. Could you give them a half-hour lesson, Lee?"

They were obviously on their honeymoon; there was no mistaking the happy glow that enveloped them.

"Wait until I put on my bathing suit," she agreed. "Give them life vests, and I'll be right back."

She flew to the office where she kept a suit for this reason. She was happy to get the job. The boy was starting to haunt her. She knew it was her suppressed maternal love stirring, and she wanted to get away from further contact with him. Father and son had wandered over to Bill and had given no indication of leaving immediately.

She quickly ran through the basic principles of handling the sails. The couple floated into the water. Using another boat, she sailed parallel with them, calling out directions as the wind carried them along.

When their confidence grew, she let the wind capsize them, then showed how easy it was to right the shell. They were eager pupils and in half an hour she let them go happily off on their own.

She had been testing the wind and now flew close-hauled into the river proper. She shouldn't. Ron no doubt had a customer for the boat, but she felt the need for wind and water to overcome the empty feeling the boy's wistful brown eyes had created.

She doubled back and forth, becoming one with the boat until conscious of nothing but the wind and salt spray. She became a water nymph in tune with her immediate world, and the elements soothed the aching corners of her heart.

One of their Hobie Cats came flying toward her. There were two on board, and while she knew the boat was too swift for her craft, she turned to challenge them, laughing joyously at the excitement of the race.

Slowly it overhauled her, and when abreast, she looked at its occupants. They were Craig and Biff. Craig was acting as counterbalance to the sails as he instructed his son at the tiller.

There was a rapt look on the boy's face, and the three exchanged happy grins as they acknowledged the carefree thrill of the moment.

Then they pulled ahead, and she turned back to the dock.

Beyond the horizon, far to the south and below the equator, the autumn breeze made the men huddle in their pea jackets. The freighter vibrated as the old diesel idled.

The captain yelled a signal, and the huge rusty links screeched as they rattled out, pulled by the weight of the anchor dropping down, down to the ocean floor.

The harbor was too shallow to enter, and the bottom shelved up too rapidly to get in closer. The native boats would have to bring the bales out. The loading would start when the sun went down. It was better that way. There would be fewer eyes to watch, fewer hands held out for payment.

He looked over the rusting hull with disgust. They were certainly digging the bottom of the barrel. Even in her best days she had been an ugly thing, and age had not softened her. As long as his engineer could keep that ancient machine together they'd make it, but it would be slow going. She was a plodding lady, an old, old plodding lady.

CHAPTER THREE

They didn't arrive the next day until noon. Bill and Lee were sitting on their favorite benches in front of the office. She was sharing her sandwiches with Bill, pausing before giving Ron a well-deserved lunch break. The weekend had brought out eager sailors.

Biff came running up to her. "We were watching you yesterday. I never saw anyone make a sailfish go like you did." He gave her a shy smile. "It looked like a butterfly dancing back and forth."

"Thank you, Biff." She laid her hand lightly on his shoulder. "You handled that Cat pretty well yourself. You beat the pants off me!"

He beamed at her praise and settled on the bench alongside her.

Craig sank into a sagging chair next to Bill. "It's Biff's birthday," he announced. "And I'm being his good fairy. He gets two wishes, and if I can possibly do it, I'm honor bound to make them come true. We do it every year.

"The first one was easy," Craig continued. "He wanted to spend the day here. I hope you don't mind. He hasn't decided on the second wish yet."

"Biff is always welcome here," Bill boomed. "And since it's his birthday, we'll let his father stay also."

"Have you decided on your other wish?" Lee asked.

"I'm thinking," he said, a small frown gathering on his forehead. "I have to make it good because I have only two weeks before I go to camp." There was no joy in his voice at the prospect.

"Morgan!" Bill barked as a dusty wreck of a car rattled down the drive. It was barely moving, which was a good thing because the owner's eyesight was failing. It glided to a stop inches away from Craig's splendid sports car.

Lee heard the explosion of breath from Craig when the expectant crash did not materialize, and she gave him a sympathetic smile.

Bill shook his head. "I'll have to work on those brakes again. He must ride without releasing the lever."

The old man managed to get out and shuffled over, giving a toothless grin in greeting. He was the proper owner of the car; they were both dusty, old, and deeply furrowed.

No one knew him as anything but Morgan, an old sea salt who haunted the docks of old-timers like Bill. They would manufacture jobs for him and slip him a bill now and then to augment his meager pension.

Cataracts were forming and the tremor of his hands was more pronounced this year, but he still carried himself with a certain dignity.

Old Morgan was a fixture and everyone would be appalled at the suggestion of putting him in a home. If nothing else, he faithfully carried gossip and, when there was a rest period, he would regale them with tales of his sailing days.

"Morgan, you're just in time," Lee said with affection. "I packed too many sandwiches, and Bill is finally watching his waistline. Sit down and help us finish them."

He lowered himself slowly into a chair and accepted the chicken sandwich.

"You make the best ones around, missy. Some of the wives are too stingy with the mayonnaise," he cackled.

Bill popped a beer for him. Morgan allowed himself three cans a day—one at lunch, one at dinner, and one before bed. Wherever he got his last meal, his friends were careful to put the extra can in his car.

"Did you hear the latest?" he said as he finished gumming his sandwich.

Biff was sitting next to him, watching him with eyes round with wonder, while Craig regarded the character with a bemused expression.

"What's up today?" Bill asked, squashing his empty can.

"Pirates!" he spat out. "Pirates are back again."

"What TV movie was that?" Bill asked tolerantly.

"No TV," he said indignantly. "It happened here. On the Chessypeake!"

Bill raised a bushy eyebrow.

"Don't believe me, huh? Well it's the truth. Jest heard it at Mer's dock. Thirty-two footer. Coast Guard caught the beginning of his call for help when he was bein' boarded last night 'n' they found a body this morning."

They all straightened in their chairs. This was news no sailor liked to hear. No matter how many boats were out, there were always times when one was alone on the empty waters, vulnerable to anyone bent on hijacking.

"Have they located the boat?" Craig asked in a tight voice.

"Nope. They no doubt needed it last night and then deep sixed it when finished." Morgan smiled contentedly. He had them sitting up now, all right!

"Are they running drugs this far up?" Craig asked Bill.

He shook his head. "I don't think the mother ship comes way up here. It usually parks at the mouth of the Bay and unloads onto smaller and faster boats. They scoot into one of our thousands of coves. You can imagine how impossible it is to monitor all of this coastline. But several fast boats have been stolen around here lately. They're getting more brazen though if they're grabbing them when occupied. Where was this boat, Morgan?"

"They were on the way to Tangier. On a cruise, I hear," he answered.

"Is that where most of it happens?" Craig asked. He was leaning forward, his dark eyes alert.

"It's ideal," Bill sighed. "There are all those small rivers

27

to hide in, and it's not far from the ocean. I guess they're using a lot of the old prohibition day tactics."

"You'd think the government agents would get all those crabbers and oystermen organized," Lee said. "They'd know if anything was out of line and could alert them."

"Bet some of them are in on it already," Morgan put in. "And you know how clannish they are down there. They're all related. No 'un would snitch on t'other."

"I guess it would be hard to watch those back roads," Craig said thoughtfully. "But the people wouldn't be as clannish as the Islanders."

"Have you prowled that area?" Bill laughed with derision. "There are lots of lanes you know nothing about. And don't fool yourself. Half of the people are related to the Islanders."

"Well, Morgan, you must keep us posted," Lee said, brushing the crumbs from her shorts. "I better get down and spell Ron so he can have some lunch. He must be starving by now."

"May I help?" Biff asked timidly.

"Of course," she smiled. "That is, if your father can spare you."

Craig waved his hand and turned to question Morgan further. He seemed overly interested in the event, but then he traveled these waters.

A small hand slipped into hers, and they trotted down to the dock.

When the weekenders started returning, the boy happily helped her empty the boats and wash them down. Craig pitched in also, though he would occasionally mutter in disgust when his cast interfered with his work.

"Do you do this every weekend?" he asked when they finally sat down. "I didn't know I was so out of shape."

Lee glanced over his long, lean frame stretched in the chair. He wasn't carrying an extra ounce of fat.

"You've been doing a lot of leaping on and off boats," she said. "And you have to compensate for the cast. It must throw you off balance."

28

"It doesn't make it easy," he admitted. "But I'm glad I had the opportunity to see what I can do.

"Biff, suppose we go for a short ride tomorrow on the *Fly Away*. I think we can attempt that. We can manage the jib and mizzen. They're small enough for us to hoist."

"Is your boat a ketch?" she asked.

"She's a beauty, Mrs. Porter," Biff enthused. "Wait until you see her!"

"Thank you," Lee laughed. "But I'll be spending my vacation with a paint bucket in my apartment."

"But you can't!" he wailed in distress. "You have to come with us!"

Lee was nonplussed at his demand.

"What are you talking about, Biff?" his father asked sternly.

"My wish, my second wish that you promised for my birthday!" he cried. His face became furrowed with the intensity of his emotions.

They all looked at him blankly.

"You promised me two wishes, and this is one you can do! I want Mrs. Porter to come along as m-mate so we can go on the cruise you promised me since Christmas!" A tear escaped and rolled down his cheek. "Oh, Dad, I so want to be with you on the boat for these two weeks! I won't see you again for a month."

Craig's face went white with suppressed anger. He was being backed into a corner to do something he had vowed to avoid. Yet he loved his son and knew how he had been building the proposed cruise into the high point of his young life.

"You can't let the tyke down," Bill's voice rumbled. "I'm with him. You promised him his second wish if it was at all possible, and this one certainly is!"

Lee saw the muscles work along Craig's jaw. His anger was palpable. He took a deep breath and turned to her.

"I honor my promises," he said stiffly through clenched teeth. "Mrs. Porter, will you be able to adjust priorities and come along as mate on the *Fly Away*?"

He saw the flash of reciprocal anger in her eyes. There

was no way she would spend two weeks in close proximity with this opinionated man. His mind was closed to her abilities for no other reason than that she was a woman.

She drew herself up as tall as she could but still had to look up at him. She glared disdainfully, picking acid words to throw at him.

"Mrs. Porter. Please, Mrs. Porter?" The hand touched hers. She looked down into the imploring eyes, and melted.

She swallowed hard against the bitter words that lay unspoken. "I'll do it for you, Biff. I'll do it for your birthday." To her surprise, the words spilled out.

"Oh, thank you!" He threw his thin body at her and hugged her. "Can we leave tomorrow, Dad?"

He was facing the water, his body still taut in rebellion at the turn of events.

"It will take a few days to outfit her, son. We have to make her seaworthy, you know," he answered, hedging for time.

Seeing that he was already sorry that he had committed himself, Lee felt a surge of reverse delight at his displeasure. She'd show him! She had deeply resented his rejection. She was as good as Bill said she was, and knew it. To be rebuffed because of her sex hit her ego. With feminine illogic, she was determined to push him into a quick commitment before he found a way to escape.

"You forget my training here. We could check out your boat tonight, and I could have the galley ready for take off by noon tomorrow. That is," she added slyly, "if you're the sailor you profess to be and have the rest of the boat in shape."

Her cutting remark hit. "She's always ready to go," he returned icily. "She's completely outfitted except for food."

"Fine," she said coolly, lowering her lashes so he wouldn't see the gleam of triumph in her eyes. He had certainly come up for that baiting! "If I'm to work the galley, I like to put in my selection of food. May I check what you have so we can order as soon as the stores open in the morning?"

Biff was beside himself with delight, completely unaware of the cold passage of words. He was going on his longed-for cruise with his beloved father after all!

"Come on, Dad," he cried, pulling impatiently on his father's hand. "Let's take Mrs. Porter now before the sun sets so she can see how pretty *Fly Away* is."

"Get going," Bill growled as Lee hesitated. "Ron and I can finish up here. Have a good sail."

He had listened to the exchange, hiding a smile at the turn the conversation had taken. They were two of his favorite people, and his big heart was happy that they were going to do what they both loved—sailing. That they were biting at each other was of small concern. Billowing sails and salt spray would soothe them. He felt a twinge of jealousy at their good fortune.

How he'd love to feel the response of a boat under his hands once more. He could sell out and get a sturdy boat and sail until his final sunset came. He'd been getting good offers for his marina.

His eyes misted. Yes, maybe one of these days, before it was too late.

"Come on, Mrs. Porter, hurry!" Biff tugged at her, urging her to the parking lot.

Craig held open the door to the low black car, his wide shoulders rigid. He was still struggling with his anger.

She paused. She couldn't ride with this stubborn man. She, too, was having second thoughts over her impulsive behavior and was now irritated that she had committed herself so easily. What had gotten into her to agree to mate for them? Two weeks with Biff's father would try the patience of a saint. Damned male chauvinist!

"I'll follow in my car," she said hurriedly. "Otherwise you'll have to drive me back here so I can pick up my car to get home. It will save time. I still have to pack."

He gave a curt nod in agreement. Biff scrambled into the car and the door slammed shut. He didn't offer to help her although he did remember to give her the name of the marina where he kept his boat.

"My slip is number eighteen on pier B," he said. He did

31

not wait until she started the car. His tires spun as he raced off.

Her eyes blazed. "What a boor!" she said as the car disappeared. "And I have to take two weeks of him? I don't know how I let myself get into this."

But she knew. The wide, innocent eyes of the pleading boy had precipitated her agreement. Her aborted maternal love had quivered in response to his loneliness. She would learn to ignore the man except for his orders as captain of the boat.

She pressed the accelerator and followed. They stopped for a light, and she caught up. She couldn't restrain a smile at the two heads so similar in the open car as they bent to each other. The sun sparked copper highlights in their thick brown hair.

As they started off Biff turned to flash her a rare smile and give a gay wave. At least one of us is happy, she thought grimly.

But she had to be honest. She was aching to go on a cruise, any cruise, and to feel the joyous freedom of wind in her hair. In order to be able to fly across the water on a long reach, she was willing to put up with the intolerable owner. He was the captain, and as crew she would have to obey his orders, but he would find her capable to equal his cold, impersonal behavior. In fact, he'd discover that she was the original ice maiden. Her emotions were under control, she felt with satisfaction.

Yet her heart skipped a beat when she saw the graceful craft sitting daintily in her slip. Her lines were in such perfect proportions that she didn't look her forty feet.

"Oh, my!" she breathed in admiration. Then repeated inadequately, "Oh, my, my!"

The grim lines on Craig's face softened at her obvious and sincere appreciation of the beauty of his boat.

"*Fly Away*." She read aloud the name emblazoned in gold leaf across the transom. "I have a feeling she's aptly named."

"I've had a six-year love affair with her," he said,

smiling. "And she's proven her name time and time again."

Biff was already on board, eagerly pulling on the stern lines so she could follow.

Craig held out his hand to assist her, but she coolly ignored the offer, leaped nimbly onto the teak deck, and walked around the rear cabin to the cockpit.

She paused as the boat moved gently under her, glancing up at the masts and taking in the trim lines. Her pulse quickened in anticipation of the days ahead.

Craig unlocked the door to the forward cabin, then climbed down to pull back the curtains and let the slanting rays of the sun enter. She followed, curious to see if the fine craftsmanship had been carried out below.

Her eyes glowed as she took in the teak and mahogany paneling. The wood had been lovingly polished, and light reflected from the soft patina. The compact galley was on the starboard side with a dinette opposite. She saw that the table top could be lowered to the seats and converted into another bunk. A head with shower, with a hanging locker opposite, partitioned the living quarters from the two forward bunks.

"They are quite comfortable," Craig said, watching her test the bed. "I put in extra thick foam mattresses. I like my creature comforts."

His anger had been siphoned away when he had seen her quick admiration for his boat. Perhaps his capitulation to his son's request was for the best. After all, Bill had recommended her without reservation, and he well knew how Biff had looked forward to the cruise. This young woman with the soft wavy blond hair and clear blue eyes could be the answer after all. It just might work out. If not, he had the option of sailing back and terminating the trip.

He left her as she began examining the galley to see what was needed. She finally emerged with a list, to find them relaxed on the cushions in the cockpit, admiring the flaming sunset.

"You have all the basics on board, so it should be easy

shopping," she said, a frown of concentration on her brow as she checked the paper.

The red glow from the sky tinted the boat with a warm radiance. The breeze lifted her short hair. Her cheeks, flushed from bending into cubbyholes, took on a soft, luminescent sheen.

"I like to have at least four days supply of food on hand," she said. "We can always pick up extras at ports of call, or are you gunk holing and only exploring coves?"

She raised her eyes to his in question, unexpectantly meeting the full force of his absorbed gaze.

"Either," he answered. "I prefer dropping anchor in quiet harbors if handy. Otherwise we'll tie up to a dock."

She lowered her lashes to hide her confusion. She had not expected that intense scrutiny. She squared her shoulders, recalling her vow on the drive over. He might be relaxing their little duel, but she still chaffed from his treatment.

"If you give me your likes or dislikes, I can buy accordingly," she requested coolly. "How efficient is your freezer?"

His eyebrow rose at her rebuff. "It hasn't let me down yet. It's dual—runs off dock current or the generator. As for food, I eat anything that is put in front of me. Biff has one weakness—chocolate ice cream—so make sure we carry it on board."

Biff had left his seat to go forward and start up the mast. The rope ratline ran to the spreaders.

"Now that the decision has been made, I'm glad for his sake," Craig said quietly. "I was feeling guilty about backing off from my promise to him."

They watched the boy's progress as he climbed happily up the rope ladder. She felt the depth of Craig's love for his son as she leaned against the cushions. The boat rocked gently as he reached the top.

The lights on the dock sprung on as the sun dipped, and the dusk hurried a darker blanket over the colored sky.

"Come down carefully, son," Craig called. "If you break a leg, the trip ends before it starts."

Lee rose as Biff returned to the cockpit. "I'd better go," she said. "I see you both have been living on board, but I still have to pack and close my apartment."

He pulled out his wallet and handed her several bills. "Will that cover your purchases?" he asked. "Also, we have not discussed a salary. What are your charges?"

She told him her usual rate.

"Fair enough," he agreed. "If you're as good as Bill says, you'll be worth every penny."

There was a restaurant situated by the marina, and he insisted she have dinner with them. They discussed a tentative itinerary. While sharing memories of different harbors, they discovered a mutual love for the Chesapeake. The hour passed pleasantly, both careful not to revive any antagonism.

"I think I'll concentrate on the Eastern Shore," he said, refilling her wine glass from the carafe. "It's still less developed than this side is."

"Definitely," Lee agreed. "There are more coves to drop anchor in, and the towns still retain the flavor of a more relaxed time."

"Plus over there the Bay is less traveled by the big freighters. Nothing annoys me more than to have to change tack for one of those big hulks."

"And they make such big waves," Biff put in, his apprehension showing.

"The Bay can do that all by itself," Craig said, ruffling his son's hair with amusement. "You've been lucky. You haven't been caught in a storm yet. We'll see how your luck holds out on this trip."

"It can be exciting," Lee offered, making light of that probability. "Testing your know-how against the elements is part of the fun of being a sailor."

Biff looked at her, doubt clouding his face. "Dad always checks the weather forecast before we go out," he declared.

"Naturally," she agreed. "All good sailors do."

"Don't worry so, son," Craig laughed. "We'll stay snug in a harbor if things don't look right."

35

Biff nodded, relieved, and plowed into his dessert—chocolate ice cream, of course.

"We'll have the boat ready to take off when you arrive," Craig said as they relaxed over coffee. "No use losing a day's sail if the wind is right."

A dreamy smile lit Lee's face. Already she could feel the movement of the deck underfoot, the taste of the salt spray. Her eyes sparkled in anticipation, and he examined her quizzically from hooded eyes.

They walked her to the car. "I'll plot courses tonight. It's all loose, though," he warned her. "The direction the wind blows will help dictate our next port of call. I want to get in as much sailing as possible."

They checked the sky automatically. A half-moon was emerging from a small cloud cover. Tomorrow looked promising.

"If we're lucky, we'll have two good weeks," she said, smiling. "I always think positive even though I know it's too much to hope for. But I'm sure *Fly Away* will take us through whatever the Bay dishes out."

"That I can guarantee," he said, closing her car door. "She's taken me through some nasty squalls with no hesitation."

"Don't take too long in the morning," Biff pleaded. "Maybe we can leave before lunch." He was so afraid something would happen before the cruise began.

"The stores don't open until nine," she warned, restraining a smile at his eagerness. "I'll rush as fast as I can."

She left, dreaming happily over the next two weeks on the lovely *Fly Away*, knowing it was far superior to any other boat she had ever sailed in. How lucky she was to have this opportunity! She went to bed, eager for the next day to start.

The half-moon emerged from behind a cloud to outline the ugly, squat lines of the freighter as it sat pulling on its anchor, slowly rising and falling with the surge of the

36

ocean. A thin, black smudge of smoke polluted the still air as deep in its bowels the diesel clanked morosely in idle.

The captain glanced at the emerging moon with annoyance, then shrugged his shoulders. Enough money had passed through the right hands to make the loading go unnoticed. He bit down on his pipe with a sardonic smile as he corrected himself. If not unnoticed, at least ignored.

He leaned on the rail and watched the parade of small boats scuttle back and forth to the mouth of the river. They came laden with burlap bags and returned empty to land. They'd be finished by sunrise, and the hull would be packed. This was his second stop. There would be one more before he started the trip north.

His eyes glistened as he pulled on the dead pipe. That was when the real stuff would come on board.

One had to admire the brains behind the setup. In a land that liked "mañana," they had built a well-run organization—well run and well oiled.

CHAPTER FOUR

After spending a fitful night, she awoke before the alarm went off. Her excitement made sleep difficult. This would be her first trip for the year. Last year she had crewed only twice and that was definitely not enough to satisfy her yearning.

The paint buckets reproached her as she ate a hurried breakfast, and she pushed them further into the corner. She could paint anytime. But sail! One dropped everything when that opportunity arose.

She shuddered over how close she had been to losing this chance because of the owner's chauvinistic attitude.

Knowing how limited the space for clothes was on a boat, she had quickly packed her duffel bag the night before. Having done it many times, she knew what essentials were needed. She now carried the bag to the car, ready to arrive at the supermarket before the store opened.

She sat chafing at the delay, camouflaging her emotions by assuring herself it was because she didn't want to disappoint the boy, and not her eagerness to test that lovely *Fly Away*—nor the challenging personality of its tall dark master.

While waiting, she turned on the radio. The local station was full of the hijacking of the boat Morgan had described, though there wasn't much more information than what he had given. The body was of a guest acting as crew. It had drifted to a shallow area off Tangier Island, where it had been recovered by a bay crabber. Death had come from drowning. The man did not know how to swim. The fate of the owner was still unknown.

She snapped off the radio. That type of news made much too despondent a note on which to start a vacation. One reassuring aspect was that a sailboat wouldn't be a lure to any drug runner. Their speed was not fast enough for them, even though a tremendous number of bales could be stored below.

Of course, no one knew if that boat had been stolen for that purpose, though the idea was on most people's minds. There was a growing traffic in stolen boats similar to that with autos. An order would come in for a particular type, and, when found, the boat would be stolen, repainted, and soon a new owner would brag about his bargain, waving his forged papers.

There was nothing new about that type of piracy—it had been carried on throughout the ages—only now they were becoming very sophisticated and well organized in their methods.

She didn't get to the boat until after ten. An impatient boy was waiting for her, and he helped empty the car trunk.

They, too, had been busy. The extra lines were off and the sail covers removed. A fresh breeze was blowing, and *Fly Away* quivered in anticipation.

"Everybody seemed to be shopping this morning," she apologized. "Just let me put the cold stuff away, then I'll help you. The rest can wait until later."

She threw her duffel bag on the extra bunk and stowed the filled boxes under the table. She had had the foresight to pack the refrigerated foods together, and was finished in short order.

She tied on her boat shoes, eager to get started. Craig evidently planned to get underway before noon.

"Which lines do you want to untie first?" she asked, waiting for his orders. He knew the current and idiosyncracies of his slip. Each boat had to be handled differently. Some docks were demons to get away from.

Biff was put in charge of the bumpers to protect the newly painted hull. They pulled out smoothly and she worked the automatic roller-reefing on the jib. The sail filled nicely. When clear of the docks, he eased the boat into the wind, and she hoisted the main and mizzen. He tailed the sheets as she worked the winch.

They worked their way carefully out of the busy Annapolis harbor. Midshipmen and their dates filled the Academy boats, gay with dress flags flying.

The senior cadets had mostly dispersed by now. The church had smoothly performed the hundreds of weddings. Happily married couples emerged alternately from the church and chapel every fifteen minutes. Outside, the visitors could gather to view the fashion parade of dazed brides and their attendants, all in their lovely wedding finery.

Lee had once enjoyed watching also, but not in the past two years. It hurt too much now. She had been one of them once.

She turned resolutely from the stark gray buildings and adjusted the sails as they changed course at each buoy. At last they were out of the Severn River, and the stronger winds on the Chesapeake caught them.

After checking the set of the sails, Craig turned off the motor. He had a sure hand on the wheel and the boat responded instantly to his touch.

This was it! This was the call of the siren that lured man back again and again to the sea.

The boat was rail down as they raced up the Bay. They passed under the twin strands of the Bay bridges, five miles of steel beauty.

Biff went with Lee to the bow to enjoy the lift and plunge of the boat. *Fly Away* was a fine lady—not too tender nor too stiff. How lucky Lee felt to have two weeks ahead of her in which to fall in love with this boat!

The wind shifted, and they scrambled back to the cockpit to adjust the sails as they went on the opposite tack.

"Where are we heading?" she asked, remembering that Craig had said the winds would dictate where they ended the day.

"The *Gratitude,* I think," he said. He was wearing the contented smile of a sailor with filled sails.

Already the boat had worked its magic on him. The tight, tired lines grooving his face had disappeared, replaced by the relaxed smile that showed strong white teeth bright against his tanned face.

For the first time Lee examined him carefully—a woman evaluating an interesting man. His slightly askew nose added interest to his strong features. He could not be classified as handsome, but she knew that if he wanted to turn on his charm, a woman would find this vibrant man irresistible. Luckily she wasn't interested; any effort would be wasted on her.

He was a strong man. The muscles rippled along his good arm and his wide shoulders spoke of power. The breeze blew the thin cotton shirt against his lean form, showing the lazy strength of his well-knit body.

His head was thrown back as he squinted to examine the set of the sails. There was a proud, if somewhat arrogant, look to him. Bill had said there was money in the family. Old money. It showed in his inbred assurance.

The wind died down, as frequently happened in the early afternoon. The pause was the result of temperatures equalizing over the land and water. A difference would appear again later as the sun heated the land, and the winds would start up again.

They moved slowly now on an even keel, and she took the opportunity to go below to make lunch.

"She's a wonderful boat," she enthused while they ate in the cockpit, balancing plates on their knees. "You must be tired. Do you want me to spell you at the wheel?" she asked Craig.

Lee didn't want to push, but she knew she wouldn't be content until she felt the boat respond to her touch. *Fly Away* was a sailor's dream.

"I thought I'd let Biff handle her while we're drifting so

41

slowly in this light breeze," he said, rubbing the shoulder of his injured arm. "The cast is a drag," he admitted, catching her concerned look.

Biff hurriedly gulped his food, eager to start. He stood behind the wheel, quivering with suppressed excitement.

Craig sat next to him with a second cup of coffee. In a quiet voice he pointed out observations to him—how to check the sails and adjust the heading, what the riffling on the now quiet waters indicated, and how the compass worked.

Slowly the boy relaxed and a grin of pure delight spread over his face as he realized that he was in control of the boat. His father was not keeping a restraining finger on the wheel as he had done the year before. He was trusting him with his beloved boat!

Lee gathered the dishes and went below to empty the boxes into the lockers. A dull pain throbbed in her chest. That was how she had pictured Big Jack with their son when he grew out of babyhood.

The wind was shifting to the west now and picking up force. After stacking the boxes to take ashore, she hurried out to see Craig reclaiming the wheel in preparation for the tack.

She showed Biff how to run out the line and to change the jib. The boat woke from her nap and kicked up her heels again. While not as challenging as the first lap, they were again moving briskly.

"Want to try her?" Craig asked.

She needed no second invitation. He moved aside and she straddled the seat behind the wheel. The room was limited in the cockpit, and his leg pushed against hers. She hid her annoyance that he did not move. Did he think he had to stay close as with Biff?

But the boat vibrated under her hands, and she concentrated on her heading. There was no room for petty emotions. She threw back her head to check the sails, exposing the long slim column of her neck. They were filling beautifully, and she felt the old exhilaration thrill her.

Her face glowed with her pleasure; her body swayed as

one with the boat. She was finely tuned to its pulse. The day was made for sailing and the conflicting emotions of elation and peace that all sailors experience while under the pull of full sails filled her.

Craig ran a critical eye over her. She certainly knew how to handle the boat, and he could relax over that. She had an interesting and mobile face, which expressed her every emotion. A smile tugged at his mouth at the happiness she exuded.

The salt air was curling her blond hair into childish ringlets. Her wide, clear blue eyes sparkled. He searched for the word to describe them. Innocent? No, she had been married. Naive was a better word. She was tall and willowy. He had been aware of her grace even when she was outfitting the boats.

She could not be classified as beautiful but was definitely attractive. Her bone structure would turn her into a handsome woman. He liked the curve of her full mouth with its promise of passion. Yet she didn't seem to be a woman fully awakened to her potential, and he wondered briefly about her husband.

All too soon, they picked up the market into Rock Hall, and she reluctantly surrendered the wheel to Craig. She had Biff help adjust the sails, and they turned up to the *Gratitude*. A long, submerged sand spit made the longer route necessary.

"Do you want to tie to a dock or anchor in Swan Creek?" he asked.

"Let's anchor out, Dad," Biff answered, and Lee nodded in agreement.

He switched on the engine as the land blanketed the wind. She dropped the mainsail and Biff helped her tie it down. She pointed out the rotting hull of the old ferry *Gratitude* that was pulled up by the docks. Many such ferry systems had collapsed with the building of the Bay bridge. A surge of nostalgia for the quiet ways that had disappeared flooded her.

They hurried to the bow and loosened the main anchor. He motored into position and called his order. The anchor submerged in the water, and the chain rattled out. He backed down until the anchor grabbed tight, then killed the motor.

The quiet of the late afternoon engulfed them. So far there was only one other boat swinging in the little harbor. The couple waved to them, drinks in hand.

The three relaxed in the cockpit, adjusting to the change from the wind and waves to the quiet, pastoral scene that surrounded them. An occasional sweep of lawn led up to large farmhouses. The muted growl of tractors plowing the fields came down to them.

"I'd better get below and see about supper before I'm too unraveled to move," Lee sighed.

"There's plenty of time," Craig replied. "There's a restaurant on shore. We can have a try at it, though today is Monday, and it may be closed."

"Put the dinghy over, Dad, and I'll row in to check," Biff offered.

"Good idea," his father agreed. "You'll get some exercise also."

They untied the dinghy carried on the back deck and dropped it overboard. They hung the boarding ladder over the side, and Biff climbed down. He soon had the oars working.

"He handles them well," Lee observed.

"He's always in it when we're in a protected harbor," Craig explained. He lit his pipe, filling the air with a faint aromatic aroma. "Good therapy. It uses up excess energy. There isn't much for him to do while sailing."

"I'm feeling him out," she said. "I'm letting him help and will increase his work load as I see what he can handle. You'll have an able-bodied seaman the next time out."

He nodded in approval. "He's eager to learn, anyway."

"You have a wonderful son, Mr. Lowell," she said softly.

He raised his eyebrows. "What brought on that bit of formality? I thought we were on first-name basis. We're together for better or worse for the next two weeks, and we may as well bury any animosity."

Lee lowered her eyes in confusion before his hard, mocking glance. So he had been aware of her irritation. She thrust out her jaw. He had started it, she thought with resentment, acting the role of a male chauvinist.

The peaceful interlude unaccountably disappeared, and she went below to her bunk. She had not had time to empty her duffel bag, so she set to work, frowning in her concentration, unable to figure out why she felt so piqued.

She heard him moving around in the galley and stiffened. She evidently was going to have precious little privacy. Perhaps she should have insisted on the after cabin, then discarded that thought immediately as impractical. Because she was in charge of cooking, it was best that she be in this section with the galley. Privacy was a relative thing on a sailboat.

As if sensing her thoughts, he came toward her and opened the doors to the head and the opposite hanging locker.

"These two doors meet and create a room for you," he explained. "If it's a hot night, I sometimes come down to get some ice cubes. So if you like to sleep in the nude like I do, you'd better keep them closed when in bed."

Her cheeks flushed. She did like to sleep without the constrictions of clothing. Wearing nightclothes because of the close confines on a boat was one part of crewing that bothered her.

He took in her heightened color and turned back to the cubes on the counter.

"The sun is over the yardarm," he said. "Time for a drink. I hope you don't want something fancy. The stock is limited."

"Scotch on the rocks with a dash of water," she answered. "I have some cheese and crackers we can nibble."

He had to place the drinks on the deck before swinging up the steps. Still, he managed well with his cast, though she observed him periodically rubbing his shoulder. It must be a cumbersome and annoying weight, in spite of the black scarf supporting it.

He adjusted a cushion and stretched out, his long form covering the seat. It looked comfortable, and she followed suit on the opposite side. She sipped her drink, resting it on her chest as she watched the lazy clouds float overhead. The sun was warm, and the gentle rock of the boat lulled her in its arms.

Strong fingers clasping her hand woke her with a start. Her eyes flew open to meet his intense gaze.

"You fell asleep," he said. "I was afraid you'd give yourself a scotch bath. You finished only half your drink."

He was so close she could see the curl of his eyelashes and the slight flaring of his nostrils as he breathed. She felt a gut wrench at the smell of pipe tobacco on his hand. The beginning of a question was forming in his eyes, and she shrank away in consternation.

She was acutely aware of the weight of his arm across her breast. He kept hold of her hand, steadying it around the glass.

His hand fell away as she lifted the glass to her lips. To hide her confusion at the sudden awakening, she concentrated on its golden depths.

"I was so excited last night about this trip, I slept poorly. Then all this fresh air today . . ." Her voice faltered in her explanation.

He reached for a piece of cheese and leaned back on his cushion. "I find it's hitting me also," he said with a muffled yawn. "It will be early lights out for us tonight."

They lifted their heads at the bump against the side. Biff was back from his trip to the shore.

"The sign says closed on Monday," he called as he held on to the ladder.

"Then I better start supper," she said, glad to go below, away from his gaze. He was scanning the shoreline, but she knew her stretched form was part of his observations.

Man, woman, and the intimacy of a boat, she thought wryly. It can be a potent combination. But she was not interested.

She had craved the give and take of male companion-ship. There had been a few dates since her husband's death, but the struggle had not been worth it. She was not a merry widow; she was a bereft wife and mother.

She quickly blocked the pain from spreading in her chest. No. It was time the mourning was over, and she busied herself with the meal, closing the door on her lost dreams.

They voted to eat outside in the cockpit. Several more boats came in to drop anchor and they indulged in the usual pastime of inspecting each craft, smugly certain that theirs was better. They also evaluated the expertise displayed in bedding down each boat. Their trained eyes easily distinguished between the beginner and seasoned sailor.

"Gee, this tastes good, Mrs. Porter," Biff said as she dished out seconds of the chicken and dumplings. "She's a better cook than you, Dad!"

"That's one job I'm happy to relinquish. And it is excellent, Lee," he agreed, starting on his refilled plate.

"All compliments gratefully accepted," she smiled. "But it won't go to my head. I know this air makes everything taste special.

"And by the way, Biff. All my friends call me Lee, and I'd like you to, if it's all right with your father."

Shining brown eyes smiled at her. "I'd like to be your friend . . . Lee," he said shyly.

"It's much easier when we have to get attention," she added hurriedly. She had to get over this desire to hug him. "My husband always said that when emergencies come up on a boat, obey orders without question, and keep them short."

"Do you have any children?" Biff asked.

She froze, afraid of the pain that question usually brought. "I had one," she answered shortly and went abruptly to the cabin. She did not see the surprised hurt spread on his face at her brusque answer.

When she came back with the mugs of coffee, she was in control again, but Biff had subsided in the corner with a book and did not look up.

47

When they finished, Craig stood up and stretched. "Son, how about ferrying us into shore so we can take a walk before going to bed? You can stand the extra weight, but I can see where Lee's cooking can play havoc with my belt size."

He jumped up, happy for the activity, and they climbed into the dinghy. It was well-balanced and comfortable enough for the three of them.

The boy eased the skiff onto the beach, and they climbed out. Craig then tied it to a tree. They found the road and walked along the quiet countryside.

"Every time I come there are a few more houses," he lamented. "That Bay bridge opened up this section and I'm selfish enough to say I'm sorry."

"I was thinking along the same lines when we passed the old hull of that ferry. I've also noticed that some of the coves Jack and I used to visit are now posted. It's sad to think why the owners were forced to do it."

They reached a crossroad and turned back. She threw her head back and sniffed the breeze.

"Honeysuckle," she sighed contentedly. "Spring and honeysuckle along the Chesapeake. My favorite combination."

He glanced at her happy face and went to the side of the road and broke off a flower cluster. He tucked it in her hair over one ear.

"In memory of a lovely day," he murmured. "I hope the wind stays with us, but with those clouds, I'm afraid we may have some rain."

"I noticed them," she said, hiding her pleasure at his gesture. "They're getting a little heavier."

"If it's too nasty in the morning, we'll hole up here or motor to a dock if you prefer."

"Never think of tying to a dock on my account, Craig. I prefer a mooring. And, as you know, it's a more comfortable way to ride out any rough weather."

"You are a seasoned salt," he had to admit. "I can see why Bill said I was crazy to turn you down. You'll have to forgive me for my reaction, Lee. I've been conditioned to expect women to barely tolerate the water. My mother became seasick even when our yacht was tied to the dock, and my wife was deathly afraid of water. She would come to please me, but I could see she was miserable whenever we sailed. So I made her stay ashore."

His face became pensive then, and, as if to stop painful memories, he gave her a mocking smile. "And later the occasional dates I showed *Fly Away* to seemed to prefer dockside entertainment."

"You evidently picked the wrong girls. But then, maybe you didn't." She gave him a wicked smile, then turned sober. It was understandable now why he had had that violent opposition in the office, and her resentment melted a notch.

They passed the small restaurant by the dock that Biff had checked for service.

"The man's gone," he said.

"What man?" his father asked.

"The one who was here before. He asked about the *Fly Away*. He thought she was the prettiest boat and he bet she was fast."

"I don't blame him for admiring her," Lee said. "There are six boats anchored out there now and, although they are nice, they all look like tubs next to yours."

"She is special," Craig said with quiet pride.

They reached the dinghy as the sun balanced on the horizon.

"Here's something I picked for you," Biff said shyly as he handed her a fistful of honeysuckle.

"Why, Biff, how lovely!" She took the tattered bouquet and swiftly bent to place a kiss on his soft cheek. "A girl always kisses a fellow when he gives her flowers," she said to cover his pleased embarrassment.

"Humph," Craig grunted as he pushed the boat into deeper water. "I've been shortchanged," he said, and his son gave a delighted giggle.

Lee put the limp bouquet in a tumbler of water when they got on board. It wasn't until she snuggled into bed that she removed the twig of honeysuckle from her hair

49

and held it to her nose, inhaling the lingering sweetness. It had been a lovely day, she mused, and her lips brushed the petals as she fell asleep.

The pumps had to work constantly to keep down the level in the bilge. The dirty water spewed out of the exhaust holes on each side of the freighter. The sun was setting, and even its golden light couldn't soften the ugly, rusting hull.

The captain lifted the pipe from his mouth and sent a stream over the side. His eyes hardened into a squint as he made out the black-hulled boat racing out to him.

The engines clanked in a monotonous rhythm, sending out just enough power to keep the freighter under control.

He nodded to the men waiting by the railing. A rope ladder cascaded down the side as the black boat pulled alongside.

He watched the man swing over the railing and brush his hands with a grimace of distaste. Two more men followed, each with a large box clutched under his arm.

Ahh. The sigh was one of pleasure, and his eyes lit with greed. This meant extra bonus money.

He ran his tongue over his thick lower lip. Already he could see the soft brown eyes melting as she handed out the gifts. One at a time, of course. They had greedy hands, but seductive bodies. He could smell the perfume, the woman scent.

He cleared his throat as he left the bridge to meet the men. His big square hulk cast a long shadow across the deck.

CHAPTER FIVE

Craig was standing in his cabin way examining the sky when she came up on deck. He was bare to the waist. A light covering of black hair made a V between his breasts. A towel was wrapped around his waist, and she remembered him saying that he slept in the nude.

"Good morning, Lee." He smiled, running a hand through his tousled hair. "What do you think the weather will be?"

She examined the clouds. "They're moving fast. It's still nice in here, but I bet it will be choppy on the Bay. If we're lucky, the rain will hold off until tonight."

He nodded. "My sentiments exactly."

"That's what the weatherman just reported," Biff called, his head appearing around his father's waist. "Hurry and get dressed, Dad. I smell the bacon, and I'm hungry!

"Dad lets me button his shirt," he said proudly. "It's hard for him to do them because of his cast."

"He's my valet among other things," Craig said, smiling fondly at his son as they disappeared into their cabin.

She wondered idly what their quarters looked like. No doubt they were in shambles with the two of them. Perhaps she should ask if they expected her to clean up every morning and remembered the constant picking up after her husband.

Breakfast was a hurried affair. They wanted to get as much sailing done as possible before the afternoon build-up of wind-tossed seas made the going too uncomfortable.

"I'm sorry to put you to the work of getting up the anchor," Craig apologized.

"It's a two-handed job," she said cheerily. "Don't worry, I've done it many times. If it's stubborn, I'll snub the line down and let the boat pull it loose.

"Come on, Biff. You have to lay out the line and chain as it comes up. The bottom is muddy here, and we'll have to wash off everything before feeding it back into the anchor locker."

They went to the bow. The operation went smoothly enough. Biff struggled valiantly to lay the line for easy sluicing.

"Put up only the jib and mizzen," Craig called as they headed slowly out of the creek.

The two worked well together by now and were shortly back at the bow. Biff scrubbed with the mop while Lee took a pail attached to a long line and scooped water to wash off the clinging mud. They had just finished feeding it down to the locker when a sharp gust of wind from the Bay tilted the boat. She made a grab for the boy as he lost his balance and rolled to the railing.

"Remember, always one hand for the boat and one for your job," she said, helping him to his feet.

His eyes were wide with the moment's panic. Seeing his white face, she put a reassuring arm around him and drew him down on the cabin top. His thin body lay trembling against her.

"Do you think your father will put up the mainsail?" she asked, making conversation to divert him. "If you were captain and it was your decision, what would you do?"

He swallowed hard as he took in the choppy water ahead. "Perhaps we should wait and see what it's like when we get out there."

"I agree," she said. "Now let's go and see what the captain tells us to do."

The poor tyke. The fall had really shaken him up. It was a near thing. If he hadn't been slowed by the stanchion post and she hadn't been fast enough, he would have rolled overboard.

They crawled back to the cockpit, clinging to the hand rails on the cabin top. The boat had a good flair, but the wind was whipping the flying spray at them.

"Get our foul weather gear, Biff," Craig said. "We'll be dripping wet at this rate. We'll wait to see what it's like outside before hoisting the main." The two exchanged grins before the boy hastened below. He had guessed right!

"Thanks," he said to Lee. His face was grim. He didn't have to say anything more. He had seen the near accident.

She hurried below for her gear, checking the galley to see that nothing was loose to fly around. It was not going to be the peaceful sail they had had yesterday.

When she came out, she saw the two struggling to fasten Craig's rain jacket. He couldn't get the cast through the sleeve, and the fit was tight over the extra bulge.

"May I help?" she asked. She didn't want Biff to think he couldn't handle the problem, but he backed away gratefully.

"The boat bounces so I can't close it," he complained.

"This must feel like a straitjacket," she said as she pulled on the material, working the snaps.

The boat lurched, and she collapsed against his broad chest.

Biff laughed. "You said one hand for the boat," he reminded her gleefully.

Craig grinned down at her. "I really don't mind you in my lap, ma'am, but it does make steering a little difficult."

She struggled up when another wave knocked her down again. She started giggling at her helplessness.

"If you find a smooth path, I might be able to get up," she cried, lifting her face from his wet jacket.

He braced the wheel with his knees and held her close as the third wave lifted them with an angry toss.

"Don't move," he ordered. "I'll be turning shortly at the

next buoy, and the waves won't hit us so hard." His head was bent over her, and she felt engulfed by his maleness.

She lay quietly against him as he angled the boat into a smoother course, then reluctantly sat up.

"It loses something with two wet slickers and a cast running interference," he grinned. His eyebrow was cocked in that mocking way of his, and she averted her face.

Had he felt the increase of her heartbeat? The rubbing of his wet suit against her cheek could hardly be reason to feel so flustered. There was bound to be physical contact while on the boat. She should follow his example. He, at least, treated the incident with humor.

She sat primly next to Biff. "If this is our course, it won't be too bad," she said evenly.

"It's straight until we duck in on the Chester River," he said. "A half-day of this will be enough." His eyes were on his son.

Following his gaze, she saw the boy's white face. She looked back at his father, and they exchanged knowing smiles.

She adjusted a cushion on the seat. "Why don't you lie down and take a nap, Biff?" she suggested casually. "It's a boring haul with nothing much to see. You'll want to be wide awake when we get there."

He needed no further urging but collapsed with a sigh, wondering what he had eaten to make his stomach feel so queasy.

"Do you mind going in our cabin?" Craig asked. "There's an aluminized blanket that will keep the spray and wind off him. It's on the top shelf in my locker."

Lee was amazed at the neat room. It wasn't at all as she had imagined. One bunk was wider than the other. It certainly must be his, she decided, and opened the locker on that side. Here, too, everything was in order—the jackets, slacks, and short-sleeve button shirts he was forced to wear because of the cast.

The cabin smelled of his shaving lotion and the faint tantalizing aroma of tobacco. She reached for the blanket.

and hurried out, overcome by the urgent need to escape the room.

She tucked the blanket around the boy. He was already asleep, his thin face very pale.

"Do you think I should turn back?" Craig asked.

Lee tested the easy roll of the boat. "I don't know," she admitted. "You know him best. Would he be upset to think we turned back because of him?"

His eyes flickered. "We'll head on. It won't take too long. I just hope you won't have to hold his head."

"You had the radio on this morning," she said after adjusting the jib. "Did you hear anything more about that hijacked boat?"

"Nothing much. It hasn't been found yet." His lips tightened. "The last port they had been to was Deal, and the marina there said they planned to go to Smith Island next."

"Then it must have been pirated somewhere in Tangier Sound."

"I assume so. I had planned to make that part of our cruise if the weather holds out. I haven't been there for a couple of years and would like to pay another visit."

The wind picked up as they passed the light at the entrance to the river. After another mile they would have some protection. Biff started moaning in his sleep, and she moved the bucket closer, just in case.

She pointed to the horizon behind them. The afternoon sun was obliterated, and the sky was a molten orange over the western shore.

"You know what that means," she said, and he nodded.

All sailors on the Chesapeake were aware of that phenomenon. An orange sky due west meant rain, and there was no way they would be able to dodge it. They were in its direct path.

"I hope we don't get too much of a blast," she said. "Still, afterwards it will be easier for Biff. The wind always swings around, and it should flatten the sea."

"I'm counting on that," Craig admitted. "It will mean a change of plans, though. I was going to go through Kent

Narrows and explore the Wye with you, but I think we'll duck into Queenstown and drop anchor. We'll do that another time."

"That's a snug and pretty harbor." She smiled, pleased he remembered their conversation that first day, and her desire to see the Wye River. "I think Biff has all he can take."

Lee had never experienced seasickness but had sympathetically observed others in that unhappy state.

The wind picked up and they flew the rest of the way while keeping a wary eye on the rapidly building clouds.

Queenstown was tucked in a picture cove, and its arms gave instant protection from the growing waves. It was like entering another world, serene and timeless, although they knew it wouldn't last long. Already the waters were receiving disturbing messages from the Bay and Craig frowned as he assessed their position. The wind would cause more of a problem than heavy seas. The low land was not too efficient a windbreak.

"I think we better put down two anchors tonight," he said, examining the clouds now approaching in a definite angry threat.

She hurried forward to untie the auxiliary anchor. It was lighter than the one they had swung the night before. Craig had said he used it mostly when on a short visit or a swim. The two together should hold them against anything other than a high gale, and this was not the season for a hurricane.

Thunder rolled, and she waited anxiously for his signal showing he was ready.

The first anchor grabbed with no problem. He then eased off at an angle so that she could drop the other one. She watched the rope play out of the hawsehole as he backed the boat to set both anchors.

The end of the rope appeared suddenly. No one had tied down the bitter end. She yelled, "Forward! Forward!" as she dived at it before it disappeared over the side.

He responded immediately by gunning the motor ahead, but a large boat can't change direction immediately, and

56

her shoulder jammed against the pulpit railing as she clung to the line.

"You crazy fool!" he blazed standing over her. "Why didn't you let it go?" He knelt over her, taking the rope from her clenched fist and snubbing it on a cleat.

"I didn't want to have to dive over and search for it," she murmured weakly through the pain enveloping her.

"So you'd rather have a broken arm," he stormed. "Of all the stupid things to do!"

She attempted to sit up but had to cry out at the effort. Her arm couldn't take the pressure. "It's my shoulder," she gasped.

A spattering of large raindrops warned them that the clouds were ready to drop their offering. Craig quickly opened the neck of her slicker and ran his hand along her collarbone.

"It doesn't feel broken, but we have to get you below deck before we're drenched. Can you hold your arm tight against your side? If it's immobilized it won't hurt so much. I'll try to help you," he instructed as he slid his arm under her shoulders.

Awkwardly because of his cast, he pulled her into an upright position and finally to her feet. She leaned against him, surprised at being dizzy.

"I'm all right now," she said, pumping air into her lungs in big gulps, desperately afraid she might faint. The raindrops increased as she managed the trip to the cockpit.

When the rocking motion of the boat had ceased, Biff had quickly recovered, and, knowing the routine, was now busily stuffing the cushions into the seat lockers to keep them dry. He wasn't aware of Lee's accident.

They hurried below as a strong gust of wind hit them. Craig slid the hatch covers closed as rain pelted down.

"We just made it," he breathed with relief. "Now let me help you out of your jacket so we can see what damage has been done."

He unsnapped the slicker, and she bit her lip as he inched it off her arm. Without asking her permission, he unbuttoned her blouse and pulled it off her throbbing shoulder. This was no time for false modesty.

He frowned at the discoloration already spreading across her shoulder. He probed with gentle fingers along the bones, then asked her if she could lift her arm.

She could. She was over the first shock and the pain was not as excruciating. They both breathed a sigh of relief at the movement.

"You're going to be one stiff girl tomorrow," he commented. "Your shoulder muscle will be doing a lot of protesting."

"I'm sorry," she said. "I reacted without thinking. A broken bone would have finished things." She hoped this would not make him change his mind about continuing the trip. "Perhaps if I put heat on it, the muscles won't go into spasm," she suggested hopefully.

"I'm trying to decide if ice would be better," he answered. "Our first-aid courses say ice should be applied first to a sprain to stop hemorrhaging into the muscles. We'll try it and see how it goes."

He placed some ice cubes in a plastic bag and draped it across her shoulder. It seemed to ease the pain, but she started to shake. The combination of the cold and the reaction was too much.

"Here's some medicine," he said, pouring scotch into a glass.

She tried to suppress the shivering, but he saw her hand shaking as she reached for the glass.

"Okay, it's into bed for you and under the covers," he ordered. "First chug-a-lug."

She drank dutifully, thankful for the warmth that spread through her.

"Now up forward," he commanded, seeing some color returning to her white face. She offered no resistance and went to her bunk.

"Turn around and I'll help," he said in a no-nonsense voice. "Your arm won't like moving for a while. Your clothes are damp, and you have to get out of them. I'll unzip and unhook things and you can take it from there."

The blouse came off, and she felt her bra unhooked. He unbuckled her slacks and pulled down the zipper.

"I knew my training would come in handy," he said with a straight face. "Now I'll let you get out of everything and into bed. I assume you have pajamas?" He cocked an eyebrow at her.

She managed a weak smile, flustered by his help. "They're under my pillow. I do own one pair for cruising," she admitted.

"Don't act modest on my account," he grinned, seeing her flushed face. "Do you need help getting into them?"

"No," she said firmly. "I appreciate your help, but please go now and close the doors. I'll manage fine."

The shaking feeling was leaving, replaced with total awareness of the man standing too close to her in the narrow space. Her breath was faster than usual.

"Look, I know how awkward it is with one hand," he persisted. "Between the two of us, we should make one decent set."

"For heaven's sake, will you go!" Her voice was shrill as she grabbed at her loose bra.

He looked surprised at the distress on her face. Teeth flashed white in his mocking smile. "I hear, oh fair maiden. Take a nap. When you wake up, we'll discuss dinner." He backed out and adjusted the doors for privacy.

Now why did she have to act like a shrew? Lee wondered, furious at her reaction. It was easy to blame it on the scotch. Following his orders, she had gulped it down too rapidly.

She winced as she struggled into the pajamas and finally lowered herself gingerly into bed, then pulled at the covers, grateful to be flat.

"Are you decent?" he asked. "We have to get this ice bag back on your shoulder."

"I'm in bed," she said.

He snapped back the doors and replaced the cold bag. Then he took the blanket off the other bunk and tucked it around her.

59

"I'm awfully sorry to be this problem," she murmured, embarrassed at his attention.

He lay a hand on her forehead and gently pushed her hair back. His face was full of concern. "If you're not improved in the morning, we'll have to hunt up a doctor and make certain nothing is broken. Meanwhile the best thing for you is sleep. With this rain pouring down we best stay put."

The rain created a muted thunder over them. She listened, letting the rhythm lull her into deciding to rest for a few minutes before getting up to dispel their worry. It really had been a stupid thing for her to do, although it rankled that his first words had so accused her.

Sometime later she was vaguely aware of the ice bag being removed to be replaced by a hot water bottle. It felt soothing, and she drifted off again. She roused at times to the reassuring sound of their voices in the cabin, but was content to drift in and out of sleep.

She awoke with a start, wondering at the reason. The bump came again, and she realized it was Biff in the dinghy.

Fingers of watery sunlight poked through the portholes. The rain had stopped. Heavens! How long had she napped? She moved to get up and fell back with a sharp cry as the pain ripped through her shoulder. He was by her instantly.

"That was silly," she said ruefully, blinking through the instant tears. "I woke up and didn't remember. I tried to push myself up with my sore shoulder."

"You're not to move," he said sternly.

"I'm perfectly all right," she protested. "I have to get up so I don't stiffen. What time is it anyway?"

"Five o'clock," he said. "I was just looking in the freezer trying to decide what to defrost for dinner."

"I mixed a meat loaf while fixing breakfast," she said. "It has to be cooked tonight. I'm not sick," she added hurriedly as he tried to stop her. "I only banged my shoulder, and I certainly can get dinner."

Reluctantly he helped her up, and she swung her feet out of the bunk. She moved her arm cautiously.

"It doesn't hurt much unless I move it suddenly. I'll have to remember to hold my elbow close to me. I should be practically good as new in the morning and be able to crew again."

She reached for a long sweater to use as a robe. On a boat everything did double duty. He sat by the table watching her awkward movements in the galley.

"In that first-aid course given us, they said to use a bandage to help immobilize an arm. Suppose we give it a try? I'll wrap it around you to anchor your upper arm to your body and leave your lower arm free so you can use it. That should help tonight while it's still so painful."

Lee agreed. She found she was reaching without thinking and the darn shoulder did hurt.

He pulled out the first-aid kit to remove an elastic bandage. He stood in front of her and suddenly looked embarrassed.

"Do I wrap it above, or, er, below?" he asked, giving her a lopsided grin.

She had to suppress a giggle. "Below. It will anchor my elbow better." It was the first time she had seen him flustered. It was nice to know he was human like everyone else. And lord knew she wasn't overly endowed!

He was inhibited by his cast, finding it awkward to control the unrolling of the bandage. She helped by slowly rotating, letting him guide its placement.

On one turn the boat rocked from a wave. Putting her hand out to steady herself, it fell against his sling, pushing hard against the cast.

"Is that too snug?" he asked, eyeing his work. Her sore arm was held securely to her side.

"No, and you're right. It feels much better being restricted."

She turned to the stove to hide her puzzled frown. She swore she had felt a hard object next to his cast inside that sling when she had braced herself as the boat lurched. Why was she certain there was a gun hidden there?

But that was silly, she reasoned. The sling made a handy pocket, and he had tucked something inside. It could be anything. She chided herself at her fanciful flight of imagination and concentrated on the meal.

"Where's Biff?" she asked as they went into the cockpit with a drink. The sun was already drying the boat, and Craig replaced the cushions.

"Getting his exercise in the dinghy," he said. "In fact, here he comes now. I see him leaving the town dock."

They watched him handle the oars. He had a good rhythm and soon pulled alongside. He scrambled aboard, showing a smear of chocolate across his mouth.

"I didn't know you had money," his father frowned. "You know you shouldn't have ice cream before dinner."

"The man bought it for me," Biff admitted. He was abashed that they knew he had succumbed to that forbidden delight. "I couldn't let it melt," he reasoned.

"It melted all over your mouth," Lee smiled, but his father remained stern.

"Since when do you take anything from strangers?"

"Aw, Dad," He looked at his bare feet, deflated by his father's disapproval. "It was the man I saw at *Gratitude*. He remembered me, and we talked about the *Fly Away*. He was real nice."

"Oh? And you told him about us?" Lee was surprised at the cold voice.

"Yes. He knows all the places we plan to go," Biff went on eagerly, unaware of his father's reaction. "I told him we were going to Wye today but the Bay was too choppy, so maybe our next stop will be St. Michaels. You did say we were going there, didn't you? He likes Tangier Island just like you do, too."

"You told him we were going there?"

"Yep. If the wind was right. He didn't believe me when I said the *Fly Away* really flies. She's fast for a sailboat, isn't she?" He was relieved that his father hadn't given him more of a dressing down. He knew he shouldn't have taken that ice cream, but the man had insisted upon buying the chocolate cone when he found it was his favorite flavor. And he really seemed impressed about their boat, asking all those questions.

Craig picked up the binoculars and started scanning the shoreline, ending at the dock.

"Is the man still there?" he asked his son.

Biff squinted into the distance. "He had a black mustache and dark red shirt and blue jeans. Do you see him? One of his arms is funny. It hangs lower than the other."

Craig concentrated on the men lolling on the dock. Two held fishing poles.

"I guess he's left," he said, lowering the glasses and ordering Biff below to wash his face before dinner.

"Is something wrong?" Lee asked when Biff disappeared into their cabin. Craig had seemed inordinately uptight during the conversation.

"Why, no." A curtain descended over his eyes. His face was blank, denying her question. "Was there supposed to be?"

She turned to go below to check the stove. She was no fool. He had tensed as he questioned his son. Also, she had excellent vision and was certain a man with a dark red shirt was still at the dock. In fact, when he saw the binoculars on him, he had quickly turned, offering his back. His left shoulder sagged lower than the right.

The rain poured in tropical fury, blanketing the windows on the bridge. The only way to see ahead was to stick one's head out of the door, and he wasn't about to do that. Thank God they at least had a decent radar on board, the only thing new on the boat. He hoped they wouldn't foster this piece of junk on him the next time.

The boat rolled alarmingly at times in the rough seas. There would be some unhappy men below. As long as the automatic bilge pumps held out, they could rest. He'd hate to depend on a sick crew to man the pumps.

Luckily they were only skirting the edge of the storm. He felt sorry for any boat caught out in the Atlantic. The weather reports said it was a demon with winds to Mark Seven.

CHAPTER SIX

The sun rose in a cloudless sky, promising a hot day. The cockpit was already warm when they sat there for breakfast.

Lee found her shoulder stiff but manageable. She was appalled at the dark bruise that discolored her skin. The sun baking it today should prove a blessing, helping it well on the way to healing by tomorrow.

After clearing away the dishes, she found the two had hoisted the sails. They hung limp in the still air.

"It was easy enough to do before we got underway," Craig said. "Biff did a good job helping me."

"I wish you hadn't done it," she said ruefully. "You may decide you don't need me."

"Don't worry," he said, starting the engine. "You can have the job back tomorrow. We'd keep you anyway just for what you turn out of the galley."

"Dad hates cooking," Biff added. "Grandma lets me help her when the cook is off, but I can't when I'm in boarding school." His face had that woebegone look that pulled at her heart. He had been changing in this trip. Happy grins were replacing the shy smiles.

They soon found that there would be no sailing that morning. The Dacron hung motionless from the masts.

Craig gave up and restarted the motor. "We'll be here all night drifting," he admitted.

"Can I put on my bathing suit?" Biff asked, pulling at his damp shirt. Beads of perspiration were forming on his forehead.

"A good idea," his father agreed. "I think we'll all feel more comfortable in one."

They left the useless sails up so that they could sit in the shade they cast. They were well aware of the burn they could get, not only from the sun, but also from the reflection off the water.

Lunch was simple—sandwiches and iced drinks. Craig insisted that Lee not cook in the heated cabin.

Biff was again allowed at the wheel. The sea was smooth, and he grinned happily now that his father moved around as if unconcerned that the boat was in his hands.

Craig finally sat next to Lee, seeking the patch of shade offered by the limp sail. The heat made them lazy as they sipped the cool drinks she had brought up.

He ran a finger lightly over the purple bruise on her shoulder. "I'm glad to see you move your arm so well," he murmured. "You mustn't be having too much pain."

"It's a little stiff," she admitted. "It looks worse than it feels."

"That was my fault," he apologized. "I told the yard to put in a new rope on that anchor and didn't think to check if the other end was tied down. I would have done it automatically, except this arm makes crawling to the anchor locker difficult, so I put it in the back of my mind as something to check when the cast came off."

His fingers continued their gentle movement, pausing at the nape of her neck. She knew she should move away. This was too much of a man's knowing caress, but she was enervated by the gentle motion of the boat and the enveloping heat.

Where was the antagonism that had sparked between them at the beginning? she wondered dreamily, leaning into his hand a fraction as it continued an exploring massage along her neck. Her pulse pounded thickly, answering the message of his long, sensitive fingers. If they were alone, she knew the pressure would increase, turning her face to meet his. The way she felt at that moment, she would find herself incapable of offering any resistance.

Biff called out, pointing to a marker they were nearing. She turned with Craig, leaning forward to check the number on the buoy. His cast moved away from his body, and she had a quick glimpse into the opening of the sling. Something dark and metallic was strapped to the cast.

Immediately her dreamy detachment disappeared. She sat upright, hiding her surprised disbelief. She had had only a fleeting view. Was it a gun—and why? She couldn't be certain. Many boatmen carried guns on board, but not on their person.

A chill went through her in spite of the heat. She knew so little about this man. Bill had known him as a young man but had admitted he hadn't seen much of him since he became a pilot.

She left those experienced fingers that had started arousing emotions long dormant, and crept to the bow of the boat. She sat, her arms around her knees, staring unseeing into the sun-dappled water.

There must be a perfectly logical explanation. When the opportunity presented itself, she would ask. Meanwhile, she would stop all this wild imagining and recapture the peace of the afternoon. It wasn't easy, and she was glad when Biff came forward to join her.

"Dad said you better get out of the sun so you don't burn. He also said if you have some ice cream in the freezer, it would hit the spot." He grinned with anticipation.

"A good idea," she said, happy to do something to dispel her somber thoughts. "Let's make root beer floats. They're perfect on a hot day like this."

They were approaching Kent Narrows now, and they sipped the soda as they carefully sorted out the maze of markers leading them through the flats. The channel eliminated the long trip around Kent Island, shortening their trip considerably.

It was a weird sensation, zigzagging the erratic course in the narrow channel, threading through the flats. If one aimed for the wrong marker, one would know immediately. Barely two feet of water covered the bottom through the dredged path. No sooner had the thought come than the boat gave a sickening lurch.

"Damn!" Craig exploded. His iced soda cascaded down his lap as he tried unsuccessfully to swerve off the edge. They looked at each other in resignation. They were aground.

"Come on, Biff," she called. "Help me rock the boat."

He responded eagerly, and they grabbed the starboard shroud while leaning far over the side. They swung their bodies in unison, trying to rock the lead ballasted keel loose while Craig gunned the motor in reverse.

For a moment they thought they were loose, but the boat only settled more firmly on the bottom.

"You know what we have to do now," Craig said apologetically. "Damn this cast. I have to ask you to do heavy lifting."

"No problem," she said while wondering if her shoulder would rebel under the strain.

The dinghy was pulled forward and tied to the bow. Biff held it steady with the oars while Craig lowered the anchor over the side to Lee. He then played out the line as Biff rowed across the channel to the other side. Lee eased the anchor out, then jumped into water barely over her knees to settle it firmly into the mud. Then they went back to the *Fly Away*. The poor boat looked distressed, as if ashamed of its plight, listing to the starboard in the shallow water.

Together they strained, hauling on the anchor line. Slowly, then with increased movement, she turned back to the channel, until with a shout from them all, she floated free.

"One thing you can be certain about," Craig declared as they caught their breath and wiped the perspiration with a towel, "I'm getting an anchor winch to do the job after this!"

A small cabin cruiser was speeding toward them, skimming high on a plane which enabled it to ignore some of the channel markers.

"Look at that fool," Craig grunted. "If they continue like that, they'll wash us back on the flats."

"They won't get far," Lee said grimly. "We still have to get up the anchor on the other side. They're blocked by our line."

She waved her arms to attract their attention and Biff did the same.

The boat slowed to a crawl as it came alongside. "What's the matter?" the man growled. "I'm in a hurry."

"That's what's the trouble," Craig answered coldly. "We had to kedge ourselves off and our anchor line would flip you if you hit it." He pointed to the now slack rope barely visible under the water surface.

The man ignored the line while busily examining the boat.

"That's a pretty craft, Captain. Better take care of it," he called back. Then, with a raucous laugh, he turned his boat around and sped back the way he had come.

Craig stared after him, a heavy frown on his face. Lee did also, but her confusion was not caused by his words. The curtain in the little cabin had moved, and she had caught a glimpse of a lean face with a dark mustache. The boat held a passenger. Why hadn't he come out, and why did an alarm run down her spine?

How odd for them to come out to this barren area just to turn around and go back. It was as if all he wanted to do was look them over.

Biff must have felt similar questions. "Why didn't he help us by bringing back the anchor?" he asked, nonplussed. He was used to the usual courtesy between sailors. "If he came all that distance to help, he could have at least done that!"

His father did not answer, and they went overboard in the skiff again to retrace their way to do that chore.

They continued on with no further mishap. Lee replaced the now melted drinks, still uncomfortable from something nagging at her about the little cruiser. Then she gasped, realizing what bothered her. The mustached man reminded her of Biff's friend of the ice-cream cone!

Immediately she backed away from the idea, reasoning that it could not be possible. If it had been the man, he would have recognized *Fly Away* and come out to talk to them.

According to Biff he was very friendly and interested in it. He had even bought him a cone. Surely he would at least have said something to the boy. Instead he had remained hidden, peering surreptitiously from behind the curtain. It didn't make sense.

They were on the approach to St. Michaels and she discarded her concern as unfounded. There was always an innocent answer to such tantalizing questions, although she would never know this one. Already the incident was fading in importance.

They were now entering the wide mouth of the Miles River. Craig lifted the binoculars to examine a group of sailboats ahead, and Lee turned to watch.

Her interest sparked upon seeing their strange shape. Multiple sails were set in an odd design. There were only five of them, and in spite of the negligible breeze, they were skimming along at an amazing speed. Craig turned the boat to get a better view of the race.

"Biff, this you have to see," he called quickly. "What luck! I've seen them race only once before. Those are log canoes right out of the history book. There are only a few left on the Bay."

Lee was instantly excited. She had read about these last remaining character boats, lovingly kept in repair by enthusiasts.

Craig explained to his son what made them so special. The early settlers had designed them to cope with the shallow estuaries upon which they traveled. Three or five logs were shaped together, and when the outsides were in alignment, they were hollowed out. They were carefully burned and scraped until a serviceable wide-beamed craft resulted. They could be poled and sailed over water less than a foot deep, carrying produce between the scattered settlers.

Unfortunately, their very shallow draft was also their biggest problem. Ballast was necessary to give them stability. This was supplied by copious sandbags. The crew was kept busy shifting them constantly as the boat tacked. It took an experienced person at the tiller to keep it upright.

This very factor now added a special challenge in racing, the only use now for the few remaining samples.

"They don't use sandbags now," Craig said. "They now rely on bodies."

Biff's eyes grew wide in astonishment. Lee had to laugh, knowing he was envisioning the crew being rolled back and forth across the bottom.

"Wait until we get closer," she advised. "You'll see what your father means."

Craig met her eyes with amusement. "See those men seemingly hanging over the side? They are hiked over the edge on boards and crawl back and forth on them as a counterbalance to the sails."

The lead boat changed its course upon reaching a marker. It now headed for them, and they had a perfect view of the mad scrambling as four men scurried off the boards placed on the starboard side. The boat almost floundered until the boards were replaced on the port side, and they again inched their way out over the water.

The boat was soon back in critical balance, and came moving swiftly toward them.

"We better get out of here," Craig said, turning *Fly Away* back on course. The river was crowded with onlookers. The race was a highlight of the Eastern Shore, and boats of all description filled the water, forcing him to thread his way carefully through the partying throng.

"I knew I should have brought my camera," Lee sighed. "That was a once in a lifetime touch with history."

Her confusion of a short time ago was completely forgotten.

"We'll be in St. Michaels in plenty of time to see if they have added anything new to the museum. It's an annual pilgrimage for us," Craig explained to Lee. "Only last year we went by car."

"I haven't been there for several years, although I've watched it grow since its infancy," she admitted. "We're lucky to have this repository to keep the artifacts of the Chesapeake. They're rapidly disappearing."

They found few boats there—most were viewing the race—and they pulled into a slip at the museum. Docking would make exploration easier. If it continued hot in the evening, they could anchor out to catch the breezes on the water.

The bold figurehead of a woman in bright blue dominated the approach. They exchanged amused glances upon hearing Biff's embarrassed giggle. The full bosomed carving was ahead of its time. She very definitely did not wear a bra under her blue draped top. As usual, there were tourists standing next to it having their picture taken with self-conscious grins.

"It started with this old house, plus the small one next door and an old shed in the back," Lee informed Biff. "It was manned by old-timers from the area, very earnest and dedicated. Half the fun was listening to the tales they were happy to tell of their youth. They could remember when St. Michaels was a busy center for boat travel. Roads were still few and in poor repair. With all the rivers and creeks, who needed them anyway!"

They explored the old octagonal lighthouse rescued from demolition as the Coast Guard replaced the picturesque lighthouses guarding the river entrances by more efficient but unromantic electronic beacons.

They marveled over the living conditions the keepers had had to contend with. The cast-iron stove and iron cots were most primitive. The huge screw which permitted the lowering of the building was still in place. Few screw lighthouses had been made, and it proved interesting to examine the mechanisms so closely.

It wasn't until they started down the steps after exploring the preserved relic that she saw him. She was certain it was he when Biff's face lit with recognition.

"There's the man who gave me the ice cream," he cried, waving to the mustached man. He evidently didn't see the boy because he turned and disappeared around a shed.

"It must be someone else who looks like him," his father said, holding him back when he started to dash after him. "It isn't likely he was the same man."

"Well, maybe," Biff conceded doubtfully.

Lee couldn't believe it. What was going on? First she thought she had seen him in the boat, and now he appeared here at the museum. There was no doubt in her mind now. Biff had been too sure of the man's identity in spite of his father's effort to dissuade him.

She had not examined him with the binoculars, yet the set of the man's shoulders, with that telltale sagging, made Biff's assertion very possible.

Still, it would be odd indeed for the man to be traveling the same route by car that they took by boat. What took them half a day by boat took only an hour or two by road.

They wandered through the new additions. They regaled Biff with descriptions of the old cannery and warehouse which used to stand there, and the mounds of oyster shells that had to be leveled to permit the new buildings.

One long shed held exceptionally fine drawings and paintings showing the beauty and sweep of the Bay area. The peaceful isolation of the salt marshes with abandoned duck blinds was a recurrent scene, one they kept viewing on this trip. This was a hunting paradise, sitting on the fall migratory route of the ducks and geese. One painting caught their special attention, and Craig copied its number. How nice it would be to even consider owning such an original, Lee thought with envy.

Lee caught Biff glancing behind him several times, and found herself doing it, also. Was he, too, trying to decide if he had indeed seen his "friend"? He must be harboring doubts, though he said no more.

It gave her an uneasy feeling, almost as if unseen eyes were watching them. She shrugged against the sensation. On a lovely day like this, there should be no room for morbid curiosity. There was no earthly reason for the man, or anyone, to be following them.

They voted to eat at the crab house next to the dock. It was a novel experience, one Biff thoroughly enjoyed. The tables were covered with newspapers, and the blue crab, which was the specialty of the house, were served directly to them on large platters, enticing and rolled in coarse pepper. Extracting the succulent meat from the shells was a full-time operation. When finished, the newspaper and shells were rolled up and disposed of in one neat package.

"Very efficient," Craig pronounced as they cleaned their hands on towelettes. "I should do that at home. One less reason to have a wife around."

Lee raised an eyebrow in derision. "There are also paper shirts, I understand, and I've seen paper sheets for beds sold in marinas. Just think, you can live a completely disposable life!"

His grin held a leer. "Unfortunately everything I would want doesn't come in disposable packages."

Oh, yeah? she grimaced silently. I bet he disposes of hearts without a second thought. She wondered why she flinched at the thought.

"I have to go into town for milk and a few supplies," Lee announced after they had finished. "Want to go for a walk, Biff? It won't hurt us to walk off some of those calories."

"I'll tag along to help with the packages," Craig offered. "I'm sure your bruised arm will rebel against weight pulling on it. We haven't been kind to it today."

They crossed the small wooden bridge leading into town, pausing to examine the clam boats pulled in the little cove. Clamming was having a resurgence, and the tasty results were shipped everywhere.

The three strolled into town. Lee was happy to see that the old buildings facing the streets were still being face-lifted. It proved the town's pride in its heritage. At one time it had prospered as an important port of entry. Then the arrival of the automobile and the resulting roads made river traffic obsolete.

73

They window-shopped along the way. As in all old towns rich in history, there were many antique stores. Lee and Biff had paused to discuss the workings of an old iron penny bank displayed in one store window, when she happened to look up. The glass acted as a mirror, reflecting the scene behind her.

Craig was leaning against a car, looking down the street. He was checking his pipe to see how well it drew. Satisfied, he put away his butane lighter. Curls of pale smoke rose over his head and she sniffed appreciatively at the fragrant aroma. Being the dinner hour, few pedestrians were abroad.

A man approached and paused next to him as he attempted to light a cigarette. He fumbled with his lighter, then asked Craig if he had a match. Craig reached in his pocket and handed the man a book of matches.

The man nodded his thanks. "Do you know where 28 Forrest Street is?" he asked.

"Sorry, I'm a stranger here myself," Craig replied.

The man nodded again and strode out of her line of vision.

It was a routine occurrence, yet Lee was surprised that Craig had matches to offer. She had never seen him use them. He always lit his pipe with a butane lighter that shot a flame into the bow. She shrugged her shoulders. It was a minor thing.

They reached the supermarket when a bright red sports car screeched to a halt across the road. A stunning woman stepped out. She was dressed in a clinging green dress that accented her alluring curves. Her pale blond hair was freshly set, and expertly applied makeup accented her slanting green eyes.

"Craig! Craig Lowell, you darling!" she cried, running across the road to them. "How wonderful to see you! What are you doing in town?"

She threw her arms around him, raising her face expectantly for a kiss.

He obliged by placing a light kiss on the tip of her nose, then stepped back from her clinging hands.

"Hello, Ruth." The mocking ring was back in his voice. "Visiting your aunt in town?"

"Yes. Aunt Dot is having one of her long weekends. Deadly dull! But now that you're here everything will be fine. You have to come over and breathe some life into it as only you can." She arched her brows provocatively. "Wait until everyone sees who I captured! There's a bunch of the old crowd down."

She ran a hand caressingly along the sling, her orange nails bright against the black cloth.

"Darling, you've been avoiding me since you broke your arm, you poor love. Did you think that would make a difference between us?" Her full lips pouted. "You haven't answered me. What brings you to town?"

"I just sailed in," he said, a small tolerant smile on his lips.

She wrinkled her nose. "That smelly old boat! Aunt Dot will have to make room for you so you can sleep in a civilized bed. If not, my room is fitted out with twin beds, one unused!" She swept up abnormally long lashes, giving him the full effect of her slanting green eyes.

Lee glanced down at Biff. He stood spread-legged, a scowl covering his face. Tight fists were jammed into the pockets of his shorts.

Craig laughed. "An almost irresistible invitation, Ruth, but I can't take you up on it this time. We take off at daybreak.

"By the way, you have met my son Biff, haven't you?" he added. "I would like you to meet Lee Porter, the rest of my crew."

Ruth ignored the boy. Her green eyes swept coldly over Lee, taking in her windblown hair and boat-wrinkled outfit. She obviously saw no competition. She nodded briefly at the introduction, then turned her shoulder, not so subtly excluding her.

"Really, Craig!" she said, not caring if Lee heard the amused inflection in her voice. "When you get tired of

75

slumming, come to the house. You remember where it is. I'll be waiting for you!"

She raised her face for a kiss. When it did not come, she patted his cheek and blew one to him before dashing back to her car.

"Remember, eight o'clock!" she called.

Lee stalked into the store. If she didn't get away, she would explode with anger. The sheer effrontery of that woman! She grabbed a carriage and stormed down the aisle.

A strong hand reached over hers and pulled her up short. "I thought we needed milk. You walked by the dairy section."

She turned blazing eyes, meeting his laughing ones.

"Wait," he cried, raising his hand in mock surrender. "Don't tear into me. You have to admit I was an innocent bystander. Besides, there are times I infinitely prefer slumming." There was a subtle change of expression as he looked into her eyes. There was nothing mocking in his face now.

"I don't like her, either," Biff said, putting the forgotten milk in the carriage.

Lee pulled in a deep, shaking breath. He was right, of course. It was Ruth's attitude that had stung her. Lee was woman enough to resent the fact that she made a poor showing next to the glamorously turned out woman. She could only come off second best in Craig's eyes. Curiously, that thought deflated her.

When they returned, she stowed their purchases in the refrigerator. It was dark by the time she climbed into the cockpit. The air smelled sweet with the odor of Craig's pipe. This was the quiet hour when the body relaxed from the stress of the day, when the mind could savor the pleasant parts and mull over the problems.

"I didn't hear the weather report," she murmured, reluctant to break the peaceful quiet.

"Biff heard it," he answered. "It's supposed to be like today with the breeze increasing in the afternoon, which will be appreciated. Perhaps we'll get in some good sailing."

"I better set my alarm if we're to leave at daybreak," she said. "What time are you planning to go?"

He stared blankly at her, then gave a chuckle. "I'm caught in my white lie. It's vacation time, Lee. We take off when the spirit moves us."

She was glad for the darkness so he wouldn't see her blush. How naive of her! He had used the excuse of an early departure to avoid Ruth's invitation. The knowledge sat warm inside her.

He slapped his pipe in his hand as he emptied the burned tobacco over the side and stood up to stretch before putting the pipe in his pocket.

"I'm going for a walk," he said, staring up at the stars. "It's a nice night. Will you check that Biff puts out his light in half an hour? I'll try to be quiet when I return and not awaken you. 'Night, Lee."

He stepped onto the dock and strode down the path into town. She watched his tall figure as he crossed the small bridge and then disappeared into the darkness.

Well, she thought with a grimace at a wave of disappointment, Ruth's invitation was too alluring to pass by after all! He could do better than her, then she admitted that she had to be honest. Ruth was a very beguiling woman. A man would be a fool to ignore so open an invitation, especially when a shared bed was included.

She rose, suddenly tired. Her arm was throbbing again. She poked her head into the aft cabin, and a tender smile curved her lips. Biff had succumbed and was fast asleep, his book balanced on the edge of his bunk.

She marked the page before placing it on the table and then turned off the radio. She eased the cover over him and, on impulse, bent to kiss him. He opened sleepy eyes. She passed her hand over his hair in a caress.

"Go to sleep, darling," she murmured. He gave a small smile before complying.

She stood a long moment, taking in the picture of his black lashes curved on his cheeks, the sweet youth of him.

There was a great sadness in her for what might have been. Then it came to her with surprise. She was not being swept with the bitter pain those memories usually brought. She was healing at last.

Quietly she turned off the light and went out on deck. She searched the sky, picking out the constellations. The half-moon shone brightly, competing with their dots of light. The three stars forming Orion's belt were above her.

Tomorrow night she'd have to check how many she remembered and maybe teach Biff a few. She went into her cabin and opened the hatch cover. The moon laid a square silver spotlight on her bunk.

She was a light sleeper and awoke when the boat tipped slightly under Craig's weight as he stepped on board. He went quietly to his cabin.

The luminous dial of her wristwatch showed that it was eleven o'clock. Mustn't have been much of a party, she thought with satisfaction, or maybe he didn't have to wait long for her to repeat her invitation. She turned abruptly in her bed and had to wince at the throb in her shoulder.

Served her right, she thought, easing her arm into a more comfortable position. None of this was any of her business.

The half-moon laid a path for the freighter to follow north. He looked up at the stars that seemed ready for picking. It wasn't the beauty that caught his eye, but the clear, cloudless night. Good.

He was far from happy with the freighter they had picked for him this time. It groaned with age and his engineer kept a string of curses blueing the air as he struggled with the huge rusty diesel. He was a good man though, now that he had finished the bottles he had smuggled on board.

He cursed as he saw the lights on the horizon. A fancy cruise ship. He was being careful to stay out of the usual shipping lanes, but those damn ships island hopped in unpredictable patterns.

He would be picked up on their radar, and again won-

dered if they reported ships sailing outside of the usual lanes to the stateside Coast Guard.

Well, there was nothing he could do now. He pulled on his cold pipe, frowning as he spat on the rusty deck.

CHAPTER SEVEN

She woke to see that she had kicked off the covers during the night. It was already hot and promised to be a scorcher. The only thing to do was to wear her two-piece bathing suit. It was not a bikini. The bottoms were abbreviated shorts, and though the suit did not flaunt, it was enticing on her slim, boyish figure.

She found it difficult to lift her arm to tie the straps behind her. After struggling fruitlessly, she admitted defeat and called to Biff. She had heard him moving in the cockpit.

"Can you tie the back of my halter?" she called over her shoulder. "My arm is still rebelling and won't bend willingly at that angle."

"Will a square knot do, or a slip knot so you can remove it easily?"

She grabbed the loose top as she whirled upon hearing Craig's baritone behind her. He, too, had decided on a bathing suit and she became acutely aware of their exposed bodies inches apart in the narrow confines of the cabin.

"Biff is checking the dinghy, so I'm offering my assistance." That mocking smile was on his face again. Was he laughing, seeing her confusion? It would be like him.

"Besides, I don't know if Biff knows his knots. It might

be embarrassing if your top let loose while hauling the sail. For you, that is."

Darn him! She'd like to wipe that smirk from his face. Instead she turned a stiff back to him, closing her eyes against the wide expanse of chest with the drift of black curly hair.

"We must be nautical," she said crisply. "A square knot will do. Now if you'll leave, I'll get breakfast going. I apologize. I didn't know it was so late. You're both up."

"We're early," he assured her, tying the straps. "The cabin was a little warm last night. If it gets any warmer, we'll end up bunking topside. I'm warning you so you don't stumble over bodies if you decide to do the same."

While making breakfast she heard the two walking overhead. She poked her head out the hatch and saw them struggling with an awning.

"I'm afraid we'll be traveling by motor today," Craig said, resting his cast on the boom. "There's not enough breeze to put up a sail. I figured the awning better go up or we'll cook."

She hurried to assist. "It's delightful in the cockpit now," she said, snapping the last rope that held the awning taut. "It will be a nice breezeway when we get going. We'll have breakfast here. It's pretty warm below."

They were finishing a second cup of coffee when the familiar red car came screaming into the parking lot. Ruth looked over the line of boats and hurried over when she located them.

This morning she wore white short shorts. Her figured blouse was tied in the front, exposing her waist and pronounced cleavage. Lee was pleased to see that there was a definite roll of fat around the tanned waist. Even so, Ruth was enticing as she came to them practicing her slow, swaying walk.

"Craig, darling," she cried, her full lips in a pout. "I took a chance that you'd still be here. I have to scold you. Why didn't you come to the party?" She stood on the dock, throwing her hips forward in a seductive movement.

81

"We all collapsed early and went to bed," he said smoothly. "In fact, we're just about ready to leave."

"Aren't you going to invite me on your boat?" she asked crossly. "I made the trip specially to see you."

"Not with those shoes," he said.

Lee winced, knowing what those high heels would do to the teak deck.

He handed Lee his coffee mug, his face expressionless. "I'll walk you back to your car, Ruth."

He stepped off as her eyes swept over Lee, taking in her lean firmness and her discolored shoulder.

"Really, darling! Since when have you gone in for a bag of bones?" she cried, her voice carrying sharply across the intervening space. She placed her arm through his, leaning her voluptuous form against him. "And that bruise! She must be awful clumsy, or have you taken to beating the crew?" She gave a hard, tinkling laugh.

Lee didn't hear his answer. She gathered the dishes and stormed into the galley. What an obnoxious female! The dishes clattered in the sink as she gave vent to her anger.

"I wish she wouldn't chase Dad all the time," Biff said, sitting in the hatchway as he finished his milk. "She's worse than all the others put together. She always wants Daddy to take her to parties. Then he comes home and is too tired to take me out the next day. When he does, she wants to come along, but she spoils it. Who wants to sit in restaurants or go shopping! She doesn't like to do fun things. If we go to a park to play ball, she sits in the car and sulks so Daddy has to stop."

Lee busied herself with the dishes. She could say or do nothing other than let him talk out his resentment.

"You should see the stupid things she buys me. What do I want with a plastic baseball bat and ball? That's for kids. I use the real thing." His frown was heavy with remembered outrage.

"Some people don't realize how quickly children grow up," Lee said lamely. "Perhaps if you let her know what you really would like . . ."

"She doesn't care," he said, his lower lips extended with

disgust. "She never talks to me unless Dad's around, and then says stupid baby talk. I don't even think she remembers my name!"

"Oh, Biff, that I don't believe," she protested. Then, in an attempt to change the conversation, she asked. "What is your name—I mean your real name? I never heard it."

"Craig, Jr.," he said, eyeing her as if that should be self-evident.

Lee had to laugh. "Naturally! You're a duplicate of your father; it would have to be. Where did you get Biff from?"

"Grandma said when they held me up in front of a mirror the first time, I pointed to myself and cried Biff. It's kind of silly, I know," he explained, suddenly shy while eyeing her warily. He must have been teased about it, she guessed.

Still, he didn't seem to mind being called by it. Was he clinging to the name, remembering the loving tone his mother gave it?

"No, I like it," she said. "It's your private name, and special."

He smiled, and never looked more like his father.

"At least you're not like some of his girlfriends, calling me Biffy or Biffy-boy. Cheeze! I don't know why he goes with them."

"Your father is a very attractive man, Biff, so women like to be with him." She didn't know how else to answer him.

"Besides one of these days your father might want to give you another mother. Wouldn't that be nice? Then you wouldn't have to go to boarding school anymore when your daddy is away flying."

"Not with that Ruth," he said with childish wisdom. "She'd make certain I'd stay in school. She doesn't want to be bothered with children."

"We're taking off as soon as you're finished talking about my marital status," Craig said coolly, looming suddenly behind his son.

Lee bit her lip. He had disposed of Ruth faster than she

thought possible. Well, she hadn't said anything that he no doubt had not heard before.

She put the last dish away and hurried to help Biff untie the lines. Craig started the engine, and they motored out of the harbor. The moving air was welcome as it was already becoming stifling on land.

Lee glanced back at the museum and gave a start. In the shade of a tree a man stared out at them. One shoulder sagged lower than the other. She reached for the binoculars to see if it was Biff's friend but when she searched for him, he had disappeared. Was he the same person? Certainly there wouldn't be two with that telltale droop to one shoulder.

She hunched her shoulders at the nagging uneasiness. Should she say anything to Craig? She looked at him and noticed the grim set to his mouth. Had he, too, seen the man?

She grimaced to herself. He no doubt was reacting to something Ruth had said. Was he sorry to leave her? They could have stayed another day if he had wanted to. They were not on a set schedule. Suddenly she was fiercely glad they were going on. Biff would be unhappy to have that woman occupy any of his father's time on this short vacation.

They relaxed in the cockpit, their long legs up on the seats. Biff was sprawled on the cabin top, reading one of the many books she had seen by his bunk. The water was smooth as a pond. No breeze was blowing to ruffle the surface. The only mark left was the trailing line of their wake that faded quickly from inertia.

"How's your shoulder?" Craig asked, breaking the companionable silence.

"Just an occasional twinge if I move it suddenly," she said, moving her arm experimentally to see the limits of motion. "This purple bruise makes it look worse than it is."

"Please don't get any more marks on you. I hate being accused of beating my crew." A grin broke out, lighting his tanned face. "And, incidentally, I don't mind looking at your particular bag of bones!"

She matched his grin. He had taken Ruth's cutting remarks for what they were worth.

"But, Craig, darling." She mimicked Ruth's petulant voice to perfection. "Why didn't you come to Aunt Dot's party? You could have had so much fun . . . Civilization . . . My bed . . . Me . . ."

He threw back his head with a roar. "I do believe I see feline claws showing!" he laughed.

"By the way, where did you go?" she asked. "The town pulls in its streets by ten, and you didn't return until eleven."

A curtain fell over his face, wiping away all trace of humor.

"I'm sorry," she faltered, seeing the abrupt change. "It's none of my business. I just wondered where the night life could be in town."

His face remained expressionless. There was no answer.

"I—I thought at the time if anything happened to Biff or the boat, I wouldn't know where to contact you," she ended lamely.

"It won't happen again," he said shortly.

She was bewildered by his sudden change. Confused, she rose and went past Biff to the bow.

She stretched out in the partial shade offered by the awning. What had she said that had made him close up so tight? Unable to figure what triggered his reaction, she gave up the riddle with a sigh and closed her eyes, letting the sweet surge of the boat beneath her lull her to sleep.

"You're going to be a lobster in spite of your tan," Craig said.

Her eyes flew open, and her hand went up quickly to shade them from the bright sunlight. Craig stood over her, seemingly as tall as the mast next to him.

"We changed course and you're in full sun," he continued. "I just realized you were asleep. You'll be cooked in short order."

She sat up and stretched. "Is Biff steering?"

"He can do no wrong here. The Bay is ours." He held out his hand to her, and she rose next to him. They held on to the forestay, looking out over the water.

"It's so peaceful when it sleeps like this," she murmured.

"And like a woman, can tear out your gut when she gets vicious."

Her glance held humor. "I can't imagine you letting a woman do that to you."

"Haven't you heard of a woman scorned?" His mocking smile was back. She had no reply to that.

His finger ran gently over her shoulder. "It's fading a little," he said absently.

"Yes, it should be gone by the time we return. Bill won't take you to task." She gave him a mischievous smile.

"Bill is quite fond of you, isn't he? I know he thinks of you as a daughter."

She nodded. "Jack, my husband, knew him before we were married. We used to love to listen to his tales of the sea. He sort of adopted me when Jack . . . went." Her voice faded. She took a deep breath, waiting for the pain to envelope her, but the surge did not come. There was only a remembered twinge of regret for what had been.

"Do you want to talk about it?" His dark eyes brooded over her.

"There isn't much to tell," she said somberly. "Jack took our son to the store. He had run out of tobacco for his pipe. There was a sudden rainstorm. I remember thinking that I hoped Little Jack wouldn't get wet. They had a blow-out . . ." She looked into the distant horizon. "The police came to tell me. It happened so quickly . . . it was all over."

He ran his hand through his hair. The muscles worked along his jaw.

"I know that bewildered feeling. One night Mary and I were planning our vacation, the next day they called me at the golf course. She had had a heart attack. There had been no symptoms, no reason. She was too young for something like that. Who would have thought it possible?

"People say such inane things—like how lucky that she had no pain, that it happened so quickly, that she would have hated to have a lingering disease." There was remembered anger in his voice.

"Yes," she agreed. She had heard it all.

They stood looking at the water, not touching. Each was alone, yet oddly close together in their shared remembrance of past grief.

She turned to him, a smile trembling on her lips. It was over. Time had finally healed her bitter wounds, and she knew she would not be decimated by that pain of loss anymore.

"How about some iced tea?" she asked.

His eyes were almost black as he looked into hers. They had shared a deep loss, and it had brought them close. Something trembled between them, something she was not yet ready to explore.

She started back to the cockpit, flustered at what she had seen in his eyes. There had been a vibrant awareness that had nothing to do with their somber confessions. And she had responded. Her heart was pounding as if she had been running.

Biff was standing proudly at the wheel. He was too short to sit and see over the cabin top.

"You're steering a nice straight course," she complimented him. "Would you like a cold soda?"

He nodded, beaming at her praise.

She mixed the iced tea, bemused over her reaction. Craig was a very masculine person with, she was certain, a long string of broken hearts to his credit. If Ruth was an example, he had to do little hunting. This forced restriction on the boat could be conducive to a romantic interlude. She paused, wondering idly how it would feel to be kissed by him. He would be masterful, she knew, bringing all his experience into his lovemaking. She smiled ruefully. It wasn't her nature to be one of many. A flirtation with Craig would leave her burned because she played for keeps, and he had no need for a permanent commitment.

No, she would keep her distance. She was hired as a crew, not a playmate, and would keep it that way.

She brought up the cold drinks and took over the wheel so that Biff could concentrate on his soda.

"Are we going through Knapps Narrows?" she asked.

"Yes," Craig answered. "There's no wind to keep us out here. We may as well take the shortcut into the Choptank."

She agreed. Tilghman Island was a long peninsula of land bisected by the canal. It saved boats traveling from the north from making the longer route around the land and its treacherous shallows extending into the mouth of the Choptank River.

"There's a fairly good restaurant at the bridge halfway through the Narrows. Want to have lunch there?" Craig asked.

"It's up to you," she answered. "It's too warm to feel hungry. How do you feel, Biff?"

"Do you have chocolate ice cream in the freezer?" he asked.

"Half a gallon," she assured him.

"Then let's eat on board."

"I bet you could eat chocolate ice cream every meal including breakfast," she teased him, and he grinned in response.

"Do you want to take the wheel now, Craig?" she asked as they approached the group of buoys at the entrance to the canal. She understood a captain's desire to steer his ship when the going became complicated. She had done it many times herself, but *Fly Away* was his pride and joy.

He settled behind the wheel. They soon felt the heat reaching out to them from the land. It must be unbearable there.

She had been conscious of him watching her since the episode at the bow of the boat, but she refused to meet his eyes. There would be no commitment made by her. They had maybe ten days of sailing ahead, and she was not going to allow her emotions to become involved in a quickie romance, nor add her heart to his list. When the trip was over, she doubted she would see him again.

They went through the narrow pass. Biff went for his camera to take pictures of the skipjacks. Their huge canvas sails were hoisted to dry. Dark bands of mildew streaked the canvas. Their numbers were diminishing, and soon those romantic looking oyster boats would be no more.

"How about a swim?" Craig asked after threading out to the wide river.

"Let's, Dad!" Biff cried happily. The heat was pushing down on them.

"Can you manage with that cast?" Lee asked in surprise.

His white teeth flashed in a smile. "It will be fanny dunking for me. But that is no reason you two can't enjoy a cooling dip." He swung north into one of the creeks emptying into the river.

"Last year I explored up here and found a small cul-de-sac. When I saw it was free of jellyfish, I stopped for a swim. There aren't many places one can do that at this time of year. Maybe we'll have luck again."

They rounded a little spit of land and entered an enchanting little cove. They examined the water but couldn't see the transparent jellyfish that were floating in most of the rivers.

"I don't know why they shun this cove," Craig said. "Maybe there's a different balance of chemicals that repels them. It's quite clear, and I didn't come down with anything after I swam here last year, so I guess it's safe."

Lee dropped the light anchor overboard, then joined Biff as they jumped into the warm water.

What bliss! She swam around the boat, then struck out to the sand spit that separated them from the creek.

She gazed back at the *Fly Away*. A flash of pleasure went through her while admiring the trim lines. Crewing on it was happiness enough, but how wonderful it must be to own it! She could well appreciate Craig's pride in the boat.

Biff was enjoying himself porpoising around the boat as

she swam back. She'd row Craig to shore so he could at least wade in the shallow area and cool off. That cast must be a demon to live with in this heat!

She pulled herself into the dinghy they now dragged behind, and called to Craig to come aboard.

"I'll take you to shore," she said, adjusting the oars. He climbed down, and she rowed him in to the small beach. Biff hung on the back, hitching a ride.

"That was selfish of me to go in first," she apologized. "All I could think of was how refreshing the water would feel, and I found myself in it."

"You're a good swimmer," he said. "You made me jealous. I'd love to challenge you to a race."

After beaching the small craft, Biff started a sand castle, and they walked along the edge, wading in the warm water.

The sun was hot across her shoulders, but the heat was tempered now by the refreshing water. They stopped when the trees crept to the edge, offering a green retreat.

"How delightful!" she cried. Her face was soft as she gazed about her, absorbing the tranquil beauty of the place. "How could I have thought painting my apartment was necessary?"

He bent his dark head, taking in her expressive face.

"We have Biff to thank for overriding my stubborn objections," he said quietly. "Bill was right. You are an excellent mate and cook."

Something in his voice caused a quiver to run through her, "Even though I'm a female?" she challenged, her laugh coming as a breathless gasp.

Their eyes met. "Especially because you're a female," he murmured.

Her nerves did a dance as his eyes explored her face, then slid across her neck to her breasts. She couldn't stop the rapid rise and fall as she fought the pounding of her heartbeat. The air was threateningly heady, the sun unbearably bright.

She smiled up at him, dazzled by the sensations swelling in her.

Suddenly they were alone, the two of them in an Eden. The sun was a warm blanket wrapping them in a cocoon of privacy while the water lapped caressingly at their feet.

Somewhere nearby a mockingbird started singing its heart out, trilling grace notes and chirps of happiness.

Yes, she thought breathlessly, that's how I feel! Her nerve endings tingled, causing a quiver to erupt in ripples through her.

Her eyes widened in disbelief over what was happening to her. The sensations were making her light-headed, immobilizing her in anticipation of she knew not what.

Though they were not touching, an electric current flowed between them, connecting them as if by wires.

His head was bent to her, his brooding eyes probing and examining. The fire in their depths lit a reciprocal one deep within her own.

"Craig." His name trembled on her lips. Had she uttered it aloud? She did not know; he did not answer.

Every feature was magnified to lay indelibly across her mind. The curled tips of his lashes, the black hairs marching across his brow, the slight flare of his nostrils as he breathed.

And his lips. His lips. She stared at them, hypnotized, waiting, longing, needing them to descend and claim hers.

The throbbing of her heart was so powerful that she raised her hand over her breast to press against its beat in a futile effort to control it. His hand rose to rest over hers, firm yet sweetly gentle. The contact fueled a further explosion of fire within her.

"Dad, Lee, come see my castle," Biff called.

She shuddered to earth, and they turned slowly in response. She found her hand in his as they splashed back to investigate the architectural marvel Biff had created.

The heat must be affecting her, Lee mused as she floated down the beach. She should get back in the water to avoid getting a sunstroke. And she had to do something about this wild beating in her.

Everything seemed a little out of focus, yet the colors were more intense than she believed possible. A languid feeling possessed her and she found it impossible to remove her hand from his. If she tried, she was afraid she'd lose contact with reality.

Not until they were back on the boat and she started the sandwiches for lunch could she gather her scattered senses.

She was acting like an adolescent with a crush on a football hero, she scolded herself. He was emitting too much chemistry. She had been isolated from men much too long.

She frowned as she forced herself to concentrate on the bread before her. He was a man with a man's desires, but he'd have to go to his Ruths. She had known passion with her husband, but her body had been dormant since the shock of his death. She had been relieved that morning to find that the desolation that had isolated her emotions was now gone. Perhaps that realization had been too sudden and her reaction extra sensitive, especially since she was in daily contact with a very virile man.

How silly it was to overreact this way! She must take precautions to keep her emotions under a tighter rein before making a fool of herself. She was determined not to fall into his arms. It would be too embarrassing for them both if later they should meet again at Bill's.

When again in control of her emotions, she brought up the lunch. She did not dare look at him but kept a running conversation with Biff.

Their damp bathing suits dried quickly in the heat. Craig let his son have a final swim before they pulled up the anchor and motored out of the small cove.

She looked back longingly at the quiet spot. Would she ever see it again? Some chemistry had started there, and she had become alive again in a very bittersweet way. At least the cold emptiness had left her soul. She would be ever thankful to Craig for that. The irrational tingle of nerves was only the result of her reawakening.

The heat was causing the air to shimmer over the water, laying a haze across the shore. They continued to motor, knowing the sails would hang useless in the still air.

"That cast must be murder," she said. He was trying to prop his arm on a pillow away from his body so that the slight breeze they were generating could cool him.

"It's ungodly how I itch underneath," he admitted. "I can't wait until we get back. I have an appointment that Monday to have it cut off."

"When will you be able to fly again?"

"I guess in two weeks. It can't be too soon for me." His eyes were following a jet trail in the sky. For a moment he was up there, his hands on a different wheel.

"The enforced idleness was driving me up a tree so I must thank you for making this cruise possible. It still isn't much of a vacation. This cast cramps my style."

I bet, she thought darkly as she ducked below to replenish their cold drinks. But the girls would think it a novelty. It certainly wouldn't keep them away if he beckoned!

He turned into the Tred Avon River on the way to the lovely town of Oxford. She always enjoyed this stopover. The quaint houses lined the tree-shaded, brick-lined streets. They were close enough to the road to be admired. The community was careful to maintain the colonial charm that drew the tourists.

"It might be too hot tied to a dock. Want to anchor out?" he asked.

"Yes," they chorused. In this sultry weather the mosquitoes could be fierce close to land. The heat would reach out to them all night, negating any cooling breeze that might stir along the water.

"I know the owner of one of the boat yards around the bend," he said after the anchor was dropped. "Let's go ashore to stretch our legs and see what he's building now."

Biff took his job as official chauffeur seriously. They climbed into the dinghy, and he rowed them in.

There were several small boat yards along the waterfront, and they turned into one. Sharp stones crunched underfoot in the rough roadbed.

"Dale and I went through school together," he explained as they walked toward the sounds of hammering and sawing. "Only he stayed with his love for boats. He inherited his uncle's boat yard and is building a good reputation for designing fast yet comfortable sailboats."

"Did he build the *Fly Away?*" she asked. "She certainly fills that category. Do you race her?"

"His uncle built her," he said. "And, yes, I did race her when I was young and foolhardy. Now I enjoy her for her comforts."

"Craig, you old son of a gun! What brings you here?" A tall bronzed man came striding out of the shed, a blueprint rolled up in a huge fist. The sun had bleached his hair and eyebrows a pale gold. "And this must be your son. You certainly can't deny him! How are you, boy?"

The men clasped strong hands, pleasure covering their faces.

"We just sailed in and are making you our first stop," Craig said. "The place still looks the same."

Piercing blue eyes swept over Lee with evident approval at what he saw.

"Lee Porter, Dale Roiden," Craig made the introductions, giving no explanation as to who she was.

He held her hand a fraction longer than necessary. "You're not from around here," he said, giving her a devastating grin. "I couldn't have missed you if you were."

She threw her head back, smiling at his obvious flattery. "I can imagine," she said dryly, disentangling her hand. "No, I'm from Annapolis."

"Lee is our crew," Biff piped up.

An eyebrow shot up as his eyes shuttered. She felt her cheeks color. She knew what he was thinking. Crew, and what else? It's mighty cozy on a boat!

She turned angrily to Craig, waiting for him to explain, but his mocking eyes were laughing at her.

"Come and see my latest effort," Dale said, leading them to a partially built hull sitting on the ways.

"Hey, she's a beauty," Craig said with approval. "Looks something like *Fly Away.*"

"She is. I dug out my uncle's old model of your boat and had it tested in the lab for water flow. I've adjusted the lines a little, and she should bring in some cups for the owner. Want to go on board?"

Needing no second invitation, they climbed the ladder and stepped onto the deck.

"We finally got the motor and hardware in and have decked her over this week." He rubbed his hand lovingly along the cabin, showing his pride in his new creation. "Come below and I'll show you the layout. It's a little different from yours."

Lee returned to the deck as the men stayed below discussing some moot point about the motor. It was a beautiful craft, and she cast an admiring glance over it, envisioning its grace when finished and afloat.

The boat was braced on the ways, high in the air. From her perch, she could see over the dividing hedge separating the boat yard from the neighboring marina.

She caught her breath in surprise. Yes, it was him. There was no denying that sloping shoulder. This was too much of a coincidence. That man must be following them!

She watched him walk to the docks, stopping to scan the boats. Was he looking for them? They were anchored around the bend, out of his line of vision. He must be going down the road stopping at every boat yard to check if they had come in.

He turned around in disgust, and she saw the black mustache. Yes, he was the same person who had pumped information from Biff.

Biff! Was he the one he was searching for? She heard Bill's words again intimating that the Lowell family were more than wealthy. In fact "filthy rich" had been his expression.

Her fists clenched in apprehension. She couldn't see Biff. He had become bored after the first examination of the boat and had climbed off.

From her height she could see the man hurrying to the road and turning into their yard.

Her mouth went dry as she scrambled over the side. Where was Biff? She had to protect him! She ran past the shed where the stranger had disappeared. Panting from

95

fright and exertion, she tore around the side, almost colliding with the man.

"You!" she exploded, too angry to be frightened now that she saw Biff was not with him. "Why are you following us?" The words flew out at him.

He drew back, startled by her blazing eyes. The force of her flight carried her on. He threw out his hands, giving her a powerful shove that threw her off balance, and fled from the scene.

She collapsed on the sharp stones, crying out at the pain as they sliced into her skin.

"Lee! Lee!" Biff screamed. Then "Daddy! Daddy!"

She was too stunned to move as tears hazed her eyes. Gravel flew as footsteps came thundering toward her.

"My God, Lee, what happened?" Craig was kneeling next to her, his hand sliding under her head. "This damn cast," he said in frustration. "Dale, for heaven's sake, pick her up!"

"She's covered with blood!" Biff whimpered.

She blinked her eyes against the tears as Dale bent over her.

"I'm all right," she said shakily. "Just help me off this bed of nails. That man pushed me off balance and I fell."

"What man?" both men asked.

Dale helped her up. Their faces were grim as they pulled at the sharp stones still piercing her skin on the back of her legs and arms.

"That man who'd been following us," she answered, looking around dazedly. He was nowhere in sight. She vaguely recalled hearing a car speed off.

"I saw him sneaking into the yard and knew he was the one I've seen on all our stops. I was afraid he was after Biff, and when I couldn't see him I guess I panicked and ran to find him. I collided with the man as I rounded this shed and he shoved me . . ." Her face went white and she started to sway.

Craig's arm went tight around her.

"You better get some attention to those cuts," Dale said

brusquely. "Come to my office. I have a first-aid kit there. Can you make it or shall I carry you?"

"I'm all right, really I am. You better let me go, Craig. I'm getting blood all over you," she said weakly, trying to pull out of his encircling arm. She didn't know if her head felt so light from the reaction to her fall or the hard, lean body she was clinging to.

"Damn the blood," he said, keeping a firm hold on her. She leaned gratefully against him as they walked the short distance to the office.

There was an old leather couch covered with papers along one side of the room. Dale swept them off onto the floor and ordered her to lie down. He reached into a cabinet and pulled out the first-aid kit.

"There's some whiskey in there, Craig," he said, pointing to the desk drawer. "I think she could stand a belt."

She felt the rim of the glass against her lips, and before she could refuse, Craig tilted some of the fiery liquid into her mouth.

"Swallow and stop protesting," he said firmly. She gagged as the raw liquor burned down her throat, bringing tears to her eyes. She looked up at him, surprised to see how gray his face appeared.

"Another mouthful and we'll get to work on cleaning those cuts," he ordered.

The second sip was just as bad. He then drained her glass, his chest expanding as the fire hit him. Dale squeezed some wet paper towels and then started daubing at the cuts on her arm.

"We'd do better if you'd stretch out on your stomach," he said. "You fell backwards and most of the cuts are on the back of your arms and legs."

She obeyed, grateful to lie down, hoping they wouldn't see her trembling. Really, it shouldn't have shaken her this badly! They went to work with the wet cloths, Dale on her arms and Craig on her legs.

"There's only one or two places that need a covering of tape," Dale grunted as they wiped at the blood. "But we'll put this antiseptic on them all. This is going to sting," he warned as he saturated some cotton compresses.

She drew her breath in sharply and grit her teeth. Biff was standing by the door, his eyes wide with concern, and she didn't want to worry him.

"I hope you've had a tetanus shot recently," Craig muttered.

"I had a booster early this year," she answered as she held herself tight against the sharp stings.

Strips of adhesive were applied and she sat up, mumbling embarrassed thanks. Her glance slid to Craig, and she smiled ruefully.

"It's a good thing someone doesn't see me now. She'd have good cause to think you've been beating me!"

A smile flickered across his face. Then he pulled on her blouse on the back of her shoulders.

"We've missed one. You'll have to take off your shirt. I'm afraid it's a deeper cut. It's still bleeding."

"I'll take care of that when we get back to the boat," she murmured, embarrassed at the thought of disrobing before these very masculine men.

He gave an annoyed exclamation. "I undressed you once. Do I have to do it again?"

Her face went bright red at the grin covering Dale's face. "He doesn't have much finesse, does he? Have you lost your subtle touch, old man?"

"I can out-subtle you any day," Craig said shortly. "She injured her shoulder the other day and couldn't bend her arm to undress. Now I have to work on it again." His eyes were back, mocking her. "Bill will kill me when I return you all battered. You're turning me into a damn nursemaid. Now are you taking it off?"

Her eyes begged him, and he turned with a sigh. "All right, we won't look. You can clutch the shirt to you like a damn virgin."

They turned resolutely, even Biff, and she had to suppress a hysterical giggle as she undid the buttons with trembling fingers. At least she had on a bra. She couldn't drape herself with the shirt after his outburst so she bent forward, her body pressed against her thighs so that he could examine her back.

It evidently was a deeper cut because they had to probe with an applicator to remove some buried gravel.

"That's some bruise," Dale whistled, seeing her discolored shoulder.

"I'm beginning to feel like a liability," she admitted, her voice muffled by her lowered head.

Craig rumpled her tousled hair, much as he did his son's. "You're excused as long as you keep feeding us like you do. We'll let you get dressed now."

She lifted her head. Their broad backs were turned, and she quickly slipped into her blouse.

"I'm not really a prude," she said. "I just didn't think my back was that bad."

Dale grinned as he closed the first-aid kit. "It's nice to see a virtuous female. One wonders at times why they bother to dress."

"I take it you're a bachelor, also," she said, smiling.

"Divorced," he said shortly. "My boats were too much competition."

Craig returned from taking Biff outside and talking to him. "Biff said he was by the docks when he saw you tearing up the drive. He felt something was wrong and ran after you. It's a good thing, because his screams alerted us. Now what is your story?"

Dale poured proper drinks this time, adding ice cubes and diluting them with water. He handed her one as they sat down, waiting for her to begin.

"I was standing on the deck of the boat and could see into the next yard," she started, nursing her drink. "I saw that same man, the one with that drooping shoulder that we saw in Queenstown and St. Michaels—the one who was questioning Biff.

"He looked like he was searching for a boat. I guess you can call it crazy female intuition, but I was certain he was looking for the *Fly Away*.

"I couldn't see Biff, and when the man came into this yard, I overreacted. I was afraid he was after Biff, and I flew up the drive to protect him. I—I remembered Bill saying your family had money, and I thought he was being kidnapped . . ."

Her voice trailed away. Saying it out loud made it all sound foolish, a juvenile's overactive imagination. She hung her head, staring at the liquid in her glass. Brother, they must think her an hysterical female!

"Shall I notify the police?" Dale looked at Craig. Their faces were serious. They weren't laughing at her.

"I daresay he's miles away by now," Craig answered. The ice cubes tinkled as he swirled his glass.

"Was he after Biff?" she asked in wonder.

There were deep lines along Craig's mouth. He looked at her as if deciding on an answer. "No," he said finally.

How could he be so certain? He drained his glass and rose.

"Shall we cut the cruise short, Lee? I can either leave the boat here with Dale and rent a car to drive home, or we can sail back tomorrow." His voice was curiously flat.

She looked at him, startled at his question. Surely there was no need for such a drastic termination to the cruise. She wished he wasn't standing by the window. His face was in shadow, and she couldn't see what answer he wanted.

Biff's voice came floating in. He was trying to entice a passing cat to come to him.

"The reason you hired me as crew was so Biff wouldn't be disappointed in losing out on this cruise," she pointed out. "I'm afraid I'm guilty of too vivid an imagination. We may as well continue. I'm certain there's some rational reason behind all this. Maybe the wind will come up tomorrow, and we'll forget all about this with a rail-down sail."

Dale's eyes were on them, questions in them which he left unasked.

Craig moved abruptly to the door. Lee had an uneasy feeling he had hoped her decision would be otherwise. Then why had he put it up to her? It didn't make sense. She rose, thanking Dale for his trouble.

"If I can scrounge up a sitter for Biff, how about having dinner with me tonight?" he asked as they went outside. "I have a date and we can make it a foursome."

"Thanks, but not this time," Craig said shortly, then continued in a milder tone. "We'll make it later when I have this cast off and can dress decently, and Lee won't be limping from her injuries."

Lee looked at him in surprise. Did he mean he was contemplating future dates? She doubted he meant exactly that. He was only being polite and using her injuries as a convenient excuse. He had no desire to double date with her, and was perhaps afraid she might construe that as a step toward a more intimate relationship.

More likely it could also be that he didn't trust anyone to stay with his son. He must be concerned after all.

She was confused now. Should she have agreed to his suggestion to terminate the cruise? She hadn't been aware how granite hard his face could be. He walked beside them enclosed in his private world.

They spent a quiet evening on the boat after dinner. She took out the sewing kit to mend a tear in a pair of Biff's shorts while Craig smoked his pipe. Her conversation was mainly with the boy. Craig seemed immersed in his own thoughts, only occasionally adding some comment, and only under direct question from his son.

"There, that's finished," she said, folding the garment. "Anything else that needs a stitch? Speak now, or forever hold your peace."

"Dad split a seam in a shirt getting it over his cast," he answered.

Craig roused himself to protest. "I don't expect that type of service!"

"And what service do you want?" she asked with a wicked gleam in her eyes. "Don't answer," she said quickly, seeing the mocking smile starting. "Go get it, Biff. I'll work as long as there's still some light." She squinted at the sinking sun.

Biff brought up the shirt, and she went to work on the seam. Her fingers started to tremble as the aroma came up from the material—his skin lotion, the pipe tobacco, and his man scent. It was a sensuous combination, and her pulse started thudding in her ears.

She managed to finish the stitching as the sun started sending out its last blazing colors. She looked at it with unseeing eyes while trying to stop the tumult within her. Carefully she folded the shirt and handed it to Biff before escaping into her cabin.

She peered at her face in the small mirror. How did it happen? Somewhere along the way her emotions had slipped from awareness of the tremendous magnetic pull of this man into love. She fought with the word. Infatuation, more likely. She wondered bleakly how long she could convince herself that was all it was.

"Something wrong, Lee?" Craig had come down into the galley and looked where she sat forlornly on her bunk. "Back hurting much? A couple of aspirin should help."

She wanted to laugh. Aspirin, indeed! She had just diagnosed a terminal illness, and he recommended aspirin!

She looked at his long fingers dropping ice cubes in the glass and shivered while remembering the feel of them kneading the nape of her neck, melting her insides to butter.

A whole bottle of aspirin wouldn't take care of what ailed her!

"How about joining me in a drink? It will help you rise above the aches." He reached for another glass, not waiting for her answer.

"It's going to be a steamer tonight," he continued. "Methinks I'll sleep above deck. I'll move the cushion on your cabin top. I need the room to brace my cast. So if you hear thumping, it will be me."

"No fair. I was going to stake it out for myself," she argued. "You said you used the cockpit."

"There's room for two." His eyes dared her.

"I'm sure," she said wryly, deliberately misinterpreting him. "Biff will be using one set of cushions, and you the other. I'm afraid my back wouldn't be happy on the hard wood."

"We can always haul up my mattress. It's almost double bed size. It would be . . . cozy."

"I'll be a martyr and stay below," she laughed.

"Don't say I didn't offer," he grinned.

What a complex man he was with his mercurial changes! One minute he was laughing, teasing, mocking, and the next completely withdrawn and untouchable.

They went up with their drinks to watch the silvery path the moon created on the water. Biff started drooping and was sent to bed with a promise that he would come back out if it proved too warm below.

She finally stood up, though reluctantly. A comfortable peace had filled her while sitting by the man. It was funny how one moment her senses would be raging, and next be in quiet repose.

"The offer still holds, Lee," he murmured into the night. "And I promise to behave even if the moonlight is hiding in your hair."

A sharp yearning flooded her, and she hurried below, unable to make a snappy retort to show him she was immune to his banter.

How silly of her to think this condition was love, she thought in confusion. She was plain lusting, and was appalled as the realization hit home.

The moon stayed in her hair as it reached through the open hatch over her bunk. The covers were pushed off in deference to the heat. Her pajamas soon felt damp. She snapped open the doors, hoping vainly for some circulation. When the movements on the cabin top quieted as Craig relaxed in sleep, she slipped out of the cloying nightclothes. That was much better, much cooler. Thank goodness he finally went to sleep, and she could take them off.

When Craig crept down an hour later to get some ice cubes for one last drink to help lure the elusive sleep, his eyes turned involuntarily to the lighted forward bunk. The square of moonlight caressed the soft roundness of her long body in silken splendor.

He stopped as if mesmerized. Then with a great effort

he climbed quietly out and back to his bed. He stared a long time into the black sky.

He gave the new course to the first mate at the wheel, and the freighter headed further out into the Atlantic. They were skirting around the Bahamas.

On many a trip he had gone in there, into the Tongue of the Ocean, unloading in the protective cover of night.

The greedy ones were ruining it. The hands were always out and they had been willing to pay off enough people in the Islands so that eyes were averted.

But the Islands were hurting. Their biggest business was the tourist industry, and it was sagging. The international papers were carrying too many accounts about the narcotic traffic there, and the holier-than-thou's were putting pressure on to clean up their Island's image. Those who used to be happy with a fair handout were now demanding more for their silence.

His bosses were too big to bow to their demands. They could move on and come back when hungry hands fell back in line. The coastline in the States was enormous and offered many places to unload.

He shrugged his shoulders. So he had to head further north this time. One place was as good as the next as far as he was concerned. He put his cold pipe in his pocket and went below.

CHAPTER EIGHT

The night had done little to cool the air. It was still hot and sticky in the morning. Lee looked in the mirror as she brushed her teeth and noted the faint shadows under her eyes. It had been a restless night filled with a tall, broad-shouldered man whose mocking eyes kept laughing at her as if knowing the torture of her body.

In deference to the heat, she reached for her coolest outfit—an abbreviated halter top and denim short shorts, then went up with two mugs of coffee.

He had removed all evidence of his makeshift bed and was sitting in the shade offered by the awning, smoking an early morning pipe.

He had on a thin cotton shirt and bathing trunks. The cotton was already clinging to his broad chest. She forced her gaze from the long, muscular tanned legs stretching across the cockpit. There were shadows under his eyes also. The hot night must have ruined his sleep too.

"Have you heard a weather report yet?" she asked. "I hope we get relief with an afternoon shower." The sky was already burnished a pale washed-out blue from the heat.

He pulled his feet in so that she could sit next to him in the shade. "I was waiting for Biff to wake up before turning it on." His eyes swept indifferently over her and on to the distance.

I know I'm not much to look at, she thought over the rush of resentment at his dispassionate glance, but he doesn't have to act as if I'm no more interesting than the seat cushions!

She turned resolutely from him, unconsciously thrusting out her chin. I know he's attracted, and I bet I could work on him with the same results as Ruth.

Her resentment floundered as she ruefully admitted that in this case it was not her physical attributes that would attract. The continuous close contact was her only ally. It was Man and Woman in a forty-foot boat. Naturally sex would rear its knowledgeable head if encouraged.

She smothered a sigh and went below to make breakfast. She had to bury these tormenting thoughts. He would never allow anything to happen between them with Biff around, nor would she.

A growing affection was developing in her for the thin, sensitive boy, and he was shyly offering his in return. Her awakening desires would have to be held in check. It was enough to know she was again capable of feeling them, and she should be thankful for that much. Besides, where were the vows she had made the other day that she was on board strictly as crew?

Craig came below to stretch a chart on the dinette table and mark off a course for the day.

"I think we'll cut across the bay to the Patuxent River and drop anchor off Solomon Island," he said, his tall form filling the cabin. "It's a short jump across the Bay at this point. If a storm comes up, we'll be heading into it, which will be the best way to ride it out. How does that strike you?"

"Excellent," she agreed, sliding the eggs on their plates. She examined him from under her lashes as he bent over the chart, lingering over the thick brown hair and striking angles of his face. There were new tension lines by his mouth.

She remembered his questions in Dale's office and hoped her response had been what he wanted. Again she wondered why he had suggested terminating the cruise. He had acted positive about the fact that Biff was not the reason for that man's odd attention.

His cast rested awkwardly on the table, the wide black scarf covering its whiteness. She should tell him that a narrow sling would give just as much support and be cooler.

Her eyes clung to the black material, then sharpened with curiosity upon seeing the outline under the material. She was right. There was something next to the cast. It didn't look like a gun after all. Why in the world had she jumped to that conclusion? She shrugged her shoulders. If he wanted something strapped to his cast, it was no business of hers. Perhaps he kept his money or traveler's checks there, she thought, bemused at the idea. It would be an ideal hiding place.

He insisted upon checking her various puncture wounds. The one on the back of her shoulder was the only dressing renewed.

"They look clean, Lee. Thank God you seem to heal quickly. Just no more injuries, please, hum?" he begged, ruffling her hair. The casual act tugged queerly at her heart.

When they pulled up anchor, she could not resist scanning the shoreline, searching for a figure with one shoulder held lower than the other. The docks were busy, but he was not there. At least she did not see him. Their confrontation must have frightened him away.

Biff joined her in their favorite spot in front of the forward cabin, where they had an unobstructed view of the sea.

"Dad said to watch out for the sun," he said warningly. They looked out on the water in companionable silence.

"Boy, would I love to jump in there and cool off!" he said finally, wiping at the perspiration on his forehead. "Or at least have a shower."

"I have the answer," she grinned, getting up. She reached for the bucket with the long line attached that they used to scoop water when sluicing mud off the anchor. She tossed the pail overboard, then hauled it up full of water.

Turning quickly, she heaved the contents over the surprised boy. He shouted with delight. After several more pails he insisted it was her turn.

The water was warm but refreshing. The two giggled as they shared some more buckets. Taking a final pailful, she carried it back to Craig.

"Stand by the scuppers and hold your cast away from you and I'll cool you off," she ordered. Biff took the wheel as he complied, laughing with them. She had to stand on tiptoe to reach over his head, then watched with satisfaction at his smile of relief.

"One more and you'll be able to face the next hour," she said, lowering the pail over the side.

She reached again, letting the cooling water cascade over his head and shoulders. She stood back as he shook his head, flicking water over the deck. His shirt was plastered to him, outlining the strong planes of the muscles across his chest.

She pulled her eyes away, not realizing that the water had done the same to the thin material of her halter top, molding it lovingly over the curves of her breasts.

He took the wheel from Biff as he went below to get a book. "I think I'll feel cooler without this wet shirt," he said. She watched him struggle with the clinging material, hampered by his cast.

She went to assist him, unbuttoning the shirt and reaching across him to pull it off his shoulder. A small rivulet of water still ran down his neck, and she ached to wipe it away. Sun sparkled on drops clinging to the hairs on his chest. Her stomach knotted with a long-forgotten pain. Her bones began melting as she fought the urge to run her hands over the tanned skin, to lay her head against its protective expanse. Her hands felt on fire where they touched his shoulder, freeing him from the shirt.

"For heaven's sake, woman, will you get me a cold beer or something!" he said huskily. "And change that damn top!"

His eyes came blazing down to hers, rendering her speechless. His face was inches from hers, his breath fanning her cheek. Her heart pounded at the force of his gaze. His hand fastened as a vise on her wrist, denying her escape. The pain became part of the spell that immobilized her. She waited breathlessly for his lips to meet hers, every fiber aching for the touch.

Biff came out of his cabin, leafing through the book in his hands.

With a muffled moan, she pulled away and flew down to the galley. She leaned against the sink, hugging herself against the pain of her desire.

This has to stop, she thought dully. He's too experienced in this sort of thing not to see how I wanted him to kiss me. And with that kiss he would have found out how completely I want him.

She drew in a long, shuddering sigh. Thank God it had not happened! She could still hang on to a vestige of her shattered pride.

She couldn't believe this was happening to her. Love with Jack had been young, gay, and lighthearted, a gentle give and take.

This emotion swamped her, shaking every fiber of her being. She knew she was standing at the brink of an earth-shattering experience, and needed to back away rapidly for sanity's sake.

This time her love would be a total giving on her part, nothing withheld, and that could leave her completely demoralized. All affairs petered out with time. Her body longed for the sweetness of surrender, to probe depths never experienced, but her head as well as her heart warned her of the consequences.

With trembling hands she removed the offending halter top, substituting a loose rough-woven shell that denied her figure. Then, conceding that she could not hide in the hot cabin, she filled three glasses with ice cubes, poured soda over them, and returned to the cockpit, carefully avoiding Craig's eyes. Not until after lunch could she relax again. Biff's chattering created a bridge they could cross upon.

The sky became an inverted white bowl, holding in the mounting heat as it drew tons of evaporating water in quivering waves. The heat became an enervating force, draining all ambition. They searched for the shade of the awning. To step out of its protection was to enter an oven. They were careful not to let bare skin touch the sun-drenched deck. To do so was to be scorched.

Lee forced herself to dip the pail overboard and sluice down the deck where they sat, creating a false sense of relief. The effort left her limp. They drank buckets of iced tea or plain water. The sweet taste of soda proved too cloying. Even Biff's young enthusiasm wilted as it became too difficult to talk.

"What say we find some rooms for tonight in an air conditioned motel, take an ice cold shower, and collapse?" Craig suggested as his strong teeth demolished an ice cube.

"I'll hold that picture before me so I can rise above this," Lee sighed. "Just imagine shivering under a cold shower! What a delicious sensation!"

Biff roused himself. "Maybe we can have room service and not have to go out even for dinner."

"If there's any available, it's a promise," Craig said, handing Lee his glass. "Just fill it up with cubes. I hope the ice is holding out."

"I loaded up at Oxford," she said, pulling at her damp clothes as she took his glass. "I'll get the ice if you stop chewing it. It's bad for your teeth."

"Yes, mother," he said straight-faced. "Any other reprimand?"

She wrinkled her nose at him and went below. She returned gasping. "You'll have to find those rooms," she said. "It's an oven below. I'd never be able to prepare a meal, far less sleep down there!" She pushed damp hair from her forehead.

After anchoring, they quickly stuffed a change of clothes into duffel bags. The hot air bounced from the streets, making walking pure torture. It was difficult to breathe.

The hot spell had driven people to the shore, and it wasn't until they reached the third motel that they found a room. Biff stopped in a draft from the air conditioner as soon as they entered while they went to the desk.

"You're lucky. We just received this cancellation, sir," the man said, passing the form for Craig's signature. "I don't believe there's another vacancy in town. We usually don't have a heat wave like this until August. We will put a cot in your room for your son," he added, smiling at Lee. "Let's see, Mr. and Mrs. Lowell? Fine. Here is your key."

Lee stiffened. Her eyes widened in shock to meet Craig's sardonic grin.

"Cold shower, remember? Only one left in town," he murmured as he placed strong, restraining fingers on her arm. "I'll be damned if I'm going back to the boat to swelter. Are you willing to face it? Besides, who'd be a better chaperone than Biff?"

"Do they have any rooms here, Dad?" Biff asked as he came over to them.

"Only one, son," Craig answered, his eyes staying on her face. "We will have to share it together."

"Hey, that's great!" he said happily. "It will be like camping out."

"Exactly!" His eyes challenged her.

Another couple came in, wilting from the heat. When informed that there were no more vacancies, the man turned to his wife in exasperation.

"That tears it, Helen!" he cried. "We go back home and climb in the bathtub. We've combed every place for a room without success." They went out, letting a finger of hot air reach in.

Lee met his challenge. "Exactly!" she answered, keeping her voice light. "Do we pull straws for who gets first crack at the shower?"

"No, we'll let ladies go first." Craig picked up the duffel bags and nodded for her to precede him. Biff ran happily ahead, already revived by the cooled air.

It was the usual impersonal motel room done in blues and greens. Two full-sized beds were against one wall.

"I prefer the king size so my feet don't hang out," Craig

said, stretching out on one bed. "I end up cornered on these. Go take your shower, Lee. Don't rush. We have plenty of time before dinner."

What delight! She let the cold, needle sharp spray run over her body, reviving her wilted spirits. This was a bit unconventional, she admitted, but Craig was right. They wouldn't be able to exist on the boat. Besides, who was a better chaperone than Biff? It was like camping out . . . Exactly . . .

When they returned from dinner, Biff's cot had still not arrived. Craig put in a call to the front desk to remind them. He dropped the phone in the cradle when finished.

"Guess what—no cots. Everybody brought their brood down to escape the heat and their supply is used up."

"Where will I sleep?" Biff asked, pressing his foot doubtfully into the carpet to test its resilience.

"You're too big to sleep in a drawer so I guess you have to shack up with your father," Craig answered.

"But you said you were too long to sleep comfortably in that bed," Lee protested. "You need the space to stretch out. Besides, your cast takes up extra room. He can use half of my bed."

A blush crept over the boy's face.

Craig saw it. Sardonic eyes swept over Lee. "Hardly," he murmured. "He's only eight, but if he's as precocious as I was at that age, he'll be climbing walls laying next to a soft young body like yours. He'll wonder what hit him!"

Her blush matched his son's.

"Of course," he continued, "since sophistication has made me immune to feminine charms, perhaps we should share the bed. Biff is a heavy but rather restless sleeper." His eyes held a speculative gleam as they traveled over her. "On the other hand, I imagine I'd become restless, also. It's the nature of the beast."

"You're miserable!" she exclaimed, not knowing whether to laugh or run for her life. "I refuse to be teased. You two will have to decide how you'll divide your bed while I wallow in mine."

They propped pillows on the beds and watched television until Biff started yawning. He crawled under the covers and was soon fast asleep. They then turned to some paperbacks picked up in the lobby.

Lee found her eyes getting heavy also and swung her legs over the side of the bed. She stretched to ease her still aching back, then stopped short. Not until that moment did it dawn on her that she had packed her case with just a change of clothes. Her lone pair of pajamas remained behind in the boat. She had assumed she would have her own room.

Craig saw her expression. "Something hit you?"

"I just remembered I forgot to pack my pajamas!" She forced the words out.

"So?" he said nonchalantly, but a gleam shot from his eyes. "I didn't either. I don't own any."

Her cheeks reddened, and she had to drop her eyes.

"Lee Porter!" She could hear the suppressed laughter in his mocking voice. "No one would ever believe you had been a married woman. I have seen the female form several times, and I assume you have seen at least one male!"

He looked at her averted face and sighed. "I assume you have on underwear. Can't they do double duty? Wear them if that will make you feel better, Miss Prim. Conventions must be upheld."

She flew to the bathroom, her cheeks on fire. He was right, of course. But she couldn't do the nude bit as he challenged, not that it had bothered her when married, but conventions were her only protection now. She had been too aware of him propped in the next bed, too overwhelmingly conscious of the long form stretched out a heartbeat away. She had been turning the pages of her book, unable to digest the print.

He was leafing through her book when she returned. "How does Joan feel about Blake?" he asked.

Her face went blank at his question.

He gave her a mocking smile. "The heroine, and the man she's bent on trapping. You're a fraud, Lee Porter. You haven't read a page!"

113

She turned her back hastily and sat on the far side of the bed to remove her sandals.

The carpet muffled his movements. He stood in front of her. "Look at me, Lee." There was velvet wrapped around the firm command.

Her eyes stopped at his belt buckle. "Yes, Craig?" she said, feeling breathless.

Strong fingers cupped her chin, raising her face until his eyes thundered into her. His grip hurt, but she did not pull away. "I wasn't able to read, either." he said. "What are you going to do about it, my moonlit nymph?"

His male scent smothered her while the fire in his eyes made the pit of her abdomen turn to jelly. His hand tightened on her face, drawing her to her feet. As if pulled by a magnet, she started leaning toward him, but his hand stopped the movement inches from his body.

"You want me to kiss you, don't you." The statement was sensuously taunting. "You want to be in my arms and feel my hands caressing you, undressing you, loving you. Shall we drown in each other? How bound by conventions are you feeling now, my hired mate?"

The words shocked her. Never, never, had a man spoken such positive seductive words to her. They ran along her nerves, alarming and thrilling her, while reducing her to a quivering mass, unable to move. She was hypnotized by the power of his voice, his magnetism, the flames in his eyes. Her body, her traitorous body, was quivering in answer, wanting, needing.

His head slowly lowered, and his breath seared her skin. An aching languor crept into her limbs and her eyes became deep blue pools. Her lips throbbed hungrily as his mouth stopped a fraction from hers.

"Please," she moaned, not knowing she had spoken.

His grip tightened. "That is what I plan to do," he whispered. "I know I can please you. And you know you don't want to wallow in your bed by yourself."

His hand released his painful hold on her chin to slip behind her head. His eyes slid to the soft waiting mouth, the throbbing pulse jumping in the curve of her neck.

A shudder ran through her when freed from the force of his gaze.

"Biff," she whispered, grasping at this last straw to regain her reasoning powers.

He tensed. "Yes, Biff," he said at last. "The chaperone."

His hand dropped, and he moved away. She wanted to cry out at the desolation that swept her. It took all of her willpower not to run into his arms and pull that dark head down, to at last feel his kiss. He couldn't cheat her out of that now! Not after setting every nerve fiber aflame.

"You've said the magic word, and you're quite safe, Mrs. Lee Porter." His face and voice were expressionless. All trace of banked passion had disappeared. "It's my turn to brush my teeth. You better get to bed if you don't want to expose me to your—er—nightclothes." The bathroom door shut behind him.

She moaned against the emotions crashing through her. How despicable of him! He had no right stripping her of all pride, playing with her as a puppet manipulated by his greater experience.

Slowly a cold anger crept in to save her shattered ego. Stonily she hung her dress in the closet and slipped under the sheet.

She heard the shower going and hoped bitterly he'd get pneumonia if he thought a cold shower was the answer.

Her body stiffened as he came out, a damp towel tied around his waist. He moved between the beds, and she braced herself, waiting to scald him with bitter words if he dared try to touch her.

Instead, he leaned over Biff to pull the unresisting boy to one side, then went around the bed to the farther side.

He gave her a sardonic smile. "I don't think Biff would appreciate being equated with a bundling board. Now if you'll turn out the light, I'll get to bed. I don't intend to sleep with this wet towel strapped around me." His hand went to pull it off.

She scrambled to obey, fuming because she knew he was quietly laughing at her.

She lay staring into the darkness, wondering how she could hold back the tears burning for release.

"Lee." His voice came softly from the other side of the room. "Forgive me? I've treated you cruelly. I'm not proud of myself. I'll behave better next time."

"There will be no next time," she said icily. "Good night, Mr. Lowell."

"As you wish, Mrs. Porter. I shall not violate your moonlit body."

Again he referred to moonlight. She was bewildered at his choice of words but was too exhausted from the emotional upheaval she had just suffered to think coherently.

What was he doing, taunting her like this? Was this how he seduced his women, trapping them in a whirl of devastating emotions? She pushed her hand wearily through her hair. She had to escape. This emotional battering was too painful.

She closed her eyes tight, willing sleep to give her release.

She woke up once from a dream where a tall dark man climbed a mast as he laughed down at her. Tears were pouring down her cheeks as he kept climbing higher and higher as the mast kept soaring over him. Suddenly he turned into an airplane and disappeared into the horizon. Her desolation was complete. She knew she would never see him again.

He pulled off his boots, dropping them by the bunk. There must have been a good storm somewhere, no doubt off Africa. The waves were high, though far apart, as if getting tired of being angry.

The freighter wallowed a little in the trough but handled better than he thought when he had first boarded her. It had been a fairly easy trip so far except for that one storm off South America.

He stretched out on his bunk, scratching through his undershirt. Hell, he could use a woman now. He grinned lasciviously. He'd have his fill when he got back. They came to him as to a magnet, knowing he spent his money freely.

They'd be waiting, all right, their full breasts pushing against him, their eyes promising anything in return for the money and gifts he bartered with.

It wasn't a bad life. He was paid handsomely for his work. He kept his mouth shut, and they timed him well. Just before the money ran out, the message would come. Another freighter, another destination. He was almost to the first rendezvous point, and the trip back couldn't come fast enough.

Damn, he wanted a woman. He pushed hard at his aching groin. He was always tormented by this reverse hunger. On land he craved a ship under him—on water, a woman.

The freighter moved on slowly, pumping up and down the long swells.

CHAPTER NINE

Craig was struggling into his shirt when she finally forced her eyes open. She reached for her watch to find it was only seven.

Before falling asleep she had sorted out what position she was going to follow. She could return home and face Bill's questions, or continue her job as mate. Her first desire was to escape. But Bill would probe until he had the whole story, and she couldn't face that. He was too genuinely fond of Craig, and did not want to cause any problem between them. She knew how protective he was of her.

The other course was to continue the cruise, drawing on every shred of pride and willpower to regulate Craig to the isolated position of Captain.

Her eyes slid tenderly to the still sleeping boy. He had been the deciding factor. There was an affection blooming delicately between them that she knew he needed. It was a child's love and that was very precious to her.

"Did the weather break?" she asked coolly.

He took in her pale face, the soft droop to her lips, and the dark smudges under her eyes. He turned abruptly to reach for his comb. She only saw the grim line of his mouth as granite eyes flicked over her.

"No," he answered. "And it promises to be another sizzler. But we don't want to spend another night here, do we?"

She bristled at the hint of derision. Holding the sheet close, she swung her feet out to the floor and reached for her slip. She pulled it on, wishing fervently it wasn't a half-slip.

She would not give him the satisfaction of asking him to turn around as she walked resolutely to the closet for her dress. She hastened to reassure herself that she was covered more completely than when in her two-piece bathing suit, but her lace-covered breasts were heaving by the time the dress clothed her. She knew he had been watching her performance with that damn mocking smile curling his lips. He would not have missed the trembling hands, the heightened color of her face.

She brushed her blond hair, wishing vainly that sailing wouldn't turn it into childish ringlets. The measured stroke returned her equilibrium, and she was able to turn a calm face to him.

"Shall I awaken Biff?" she asked. Was that her voice so cool and composed while every part of her churned? "If we're continuing on, we better get going, don't you think? It's bound to be more tolerable on the water than on the land, even though the weather forecast last night announced a record breaking 100."

The large hand moved gently across the boy's shoulder. Bitterly she thought of the difference between his treatment of his son and a woman. He had been just as damnably assured of Ruth as he was of her. And all she wanted was one gentle touch, one glance of affection like he gave to his son.

She turned briskly to repack her bag. This was not the attitude she had decreed for herself last night. He had unleashed a wantonness in her she had never known existed. She knew Craig's arms could plunge her into depths and heights and she closed her mind resolutely. She would stay out of the reach of those arms and avoid those consuming flames that burned deep in his eyes . . . and would remain safe. It was a cool and collected young lady that walked with them to the dining room for breakfast.

Heat mirages already shimmered off the streets when they left the motel. They stopped short at the physical impact of the hot air as it hit them after leaving the air conditioned building.

"Do we have to go?" Biff faltered, gazing longingly at the motel.

"You wanted the cruise, so no complaints," his father answered. "Besides, I was informed that the room was available only for the one night. Let's get moving so we can get off these damn streets and into our bathing suits."

When they reached the marina, he stopped at the office. "Come in out of the sun while I check the weather forecast and make a call."

They followed him in, happy for the respite in the cooled room. They were already gasping after that short exposure.

Craig spoke briefly to the young woman at the desk and was pointed to a door. He went in, closing the door behind him, but not before Lee caught a glimpse of a vaguely familiar face. She shrugged. Perhaps he had been to Bill's. Marina owners had a habit of stopping in to check out other ones. It was a well-known occupational disease.

She spent a half-hour entertaining Biff, surprised at the length of time necessary to get the forecast. At least he had been considerate enough to park them in this office. The Navy Air Force base was close by, and they watched from the window as lethal looking fighter planes maneuvered over the water.

A subdued murmur of voices kept coming from the room. Craig must have moved near the door because she could now hear the cold anger in his voice. The door finally opened. He came out, his face grim.

"Is something wrong?" she asked in alarm.

A curtain descended swiftly, blanking his face. "No. Is there supposed to be?"

She dropped her lashes to hide her quick hurt at the re-

120

buff. She doubted she had imagined his anger. She was too exquisitely attuned to his voice and moods by now.

"They don't hold out much hope for relief for the next twenty-four hours," he said as he picked up the duffel bags. "It will be hot going. Tonight we suffer unless we can get rooms again. Two rooms," he added with emphasis.

"Don't let me put you out if there is only one," she said stiffly. "I wouldn't deprive you and Biff. After all, I am only the crew!"

"Don't be bitchy," he said curtly, opening the door to the heat, and they plunged out to meet it.

There was a modicum of breeze that was greatly appreciated when they reached the Chesapeake. It did not last long though as the brassy sun took over. Soon rivulets of perspiration ran down their bodies.

Lee set up an hourly routine with Biff. The bucket lifted pails of water to sluice down the deck where they sat, then they gratefully doused each other. She let Biff have the fun of pouring the water over his father.

Keep away, she reminded herself.

The slant of the sun dictated which side of the cockpit the awning protected, and she made certain Biff was between them when they lined up on the port or starboard side. Craig's arm must not reach out with those long fingers to massage her neck, melting her very marrow.

If possible, it was hotter than the day before. No breeze now touched the glassy water. They ate little, the heat effectively destroying their appetites, though Lee insisted that they nibble on saltines and salted nuts to replenish their sodium level.

Her words were short and stilted when she had to speak to Craig. He answered in cool monosyllables. Biff's eyes went from one to the other and, as the morning wore on, his bewilderment became more pronounced. Finally after she gave a particularly clipped response to a question from his father, he turned to her.

"Is something wrong, Lee? Did I do something?" he questioned. Her heart lurched at the sweet, perplexed face.

121

Her eyes flew to the man behind the wheel, meeting his stony face.

Then the mocking eyebrow went up; the corner of his mouth gave a quirk. "Truce?" he asked.

Her lips tightened in rebellion. He was the cause of this impasse. It would be far better to keep things at this frigid level!

A small hand touched her arm, and she softened helplessly as she met his beseeching eyes. "It's nothing, Biff," she said, smiling at him. "The heat must be getting to us."

She rose to collect their glasses, then, looking defiantly at the father, she murmured, "Truce. For Biff."

He adjusted the course and let Biff have the wheel. "When this breaks, it's going to be one hell of a storm," he commented.

"And I hope we're in a safe port," Lee added fervently. "This Bay can be vicious."

"I know," he replied, crunching on an ice cube. "I've been caught in some."

They described to Biff how to meet a storm. It was easier after that, and they conversed normally as they continued south.

"Where are we heading today?" Lee asked.

"I was going to sail down to Smith Island and enter from the west, but I don't trust this weather. If we get the promised storm, there are no coves to run to for protection. We'll angle in through Hooper Strait and continue south inside the islands. They're too low to protect us from high winds, but at least they'll break the build up of the waves. We'll also be more likely to find a harbor to run to on the mainland."

They lunched on cold jellied consomme and saltines, Lee ever conscious of the salt they were losing.

She was happy to point out the nesting ospreys to Biff. The birds were making a remarkable comeback after being nearly decimated by DDT. Tall poles with platforms on top offered tempting nesting sites. They had been placed in the marshy islands by concerned bird and conservation organizations.

The searing heat became worse, completely devitalizing them as they motored around Sharkfin Light and headed past Deal and South Marsh Islands. The low islands shimmered in the heat waves.

"We'll duck into Crisfield and replenish our supplies for the return trip," Craig decided. "We're also more likely to find a decent motel. With two rooms." His eyes crinkled.

"Truce," she reminded him.

"Truce," he agreed. "That one slipped out."

He lifted his foot on the seat to rest his cast on his bent knee. Her nerves convoluted upon seeing the rippling of his thigh muscles. She hastily took an ice cube to moisten her dry mouth.

God, I'm lusting! she groaned inwardly. I'll never last the trip torturing myself like this! She looked bleakly at the wavering shoreline.

The humidity pressed down, robbing them again of the desire to talk. It lay like a smothering blanket, oppressing and debilitating, a foretaste of Hades. Despite her lethargy, Lee was aware of the man now brooding and withdrawn. She had reached the point where she quivered to every nuance of change in him.

They were forced to wear sunglasses against the hot glare bouncing from the glassy waters. Even so, she was aware that he was examining minutely every boat they passed. The crabbers increased in numbers. They were now in the middle of the home of the Maryland crab. The lone men ran slowly along their crab lines. In practiced rhythm they swung the traps on board, knocked out the clinging crustaceans, replaced the bait, and dropped everything overboard before putting slowly to the next trap being lifted by a rotating drum. It must be murder working like that in this heat, but they went on as if immune.

"In shallow water where they can be seen swimming, they use hand scoops to catch the crabs," Lee informed Biff, noticing his interest. "Crabbing and oystering are the main source of income to the Islanders. The processing

123

factories are on the mainland. If it wasn't so hot, it would be interesting to watch one when we get in."

"Stop your chattering, woman," Craig said tersely.

She froze, surprised at the unwarranted command. His face was cold and grim, his eyes unreadable behind the reflections bouncing off the sunglasses. She fumed at his uncalled for reprimand and opened her mouth to make a scathing reply.

"Get me some ice cubes," he said, cutting her short. Then, seeing her blazing eyes, he added, "Please." His voice sounded suddenly unbearably weary, but there was no apology for his caustic words.

She went to comply, her back stiff with anger. How easily he regulated her to the position of hired crew when his male interests weren't aroused. She wouldn't play games with him last night so he had no more use for her except as a servant.

But wasn't that what she had wanted? It would make it easier for her to block him out of her thoughts . . . and heart. She stared out of the porthole, confused by her conflicting thoughts until the heat drove her out.

She handed him the cup of ice cubes, stonily avoiding looking at him. Taking the bucket forward, she cooled a portion of the deck by the mast with pails of water. She then draped a beach towel over the boom and sat in the small square of shade it offered. Her anger was so raw she could not face sitting next to him in the cockpit.

Biff came to her. "Can I get you some iced tea?" he asked, not able to hide his worried expression. He was back to the shy lonely boy she had first met.

"Thank you, Biff, but I'm all right," she said, her voice soft with affection. "I thought I'd try a new position. It's crowded in the cockpit."

"Dad . . . Dad is upset about something," he said, his lower lip quivering. "He says things he doesn't mean when he's worried." He looked at her earnestly, willing her to forgive his god.

Her hand went to his shoulder with compassion. How

124

she longed to hug him and reassure him with a mother's love!

"I understand, dear." The endearment slipped out. "This heat is getting to us all. I'll stay here for a while, if you don't mind. And you better get back in the shade. This towel doesn't create enough for two."

He nodded his head solemnly and left. She bent her knees under her chin to avoid the scorch of the sun, and leaned wearily against the mast.

What a miserable turn her life had taken. She had finally emerged from the loss of her husband and son to be plunged into another grief-filled pit over a man whose only use for a woman was his own gratification.

She winced, remembering his taunting, sensuous words of the night before as he whipped her with his knowledge of her desire. The horrible part was that she had stood there helplessly taking it, her bones melting with physical need for him. She had never felt so debased, so incapable of handling a situation.

She strove to stir the angry resentment again so that she could reclaim her pride. Again she felt his breath fanning her cheek, his mouth poised a hair's-breadth from her yearning lips, and her heart cried.

She sat huddled by the mast until they picked up the markers into Little Annemessex River leading to Crisfield.

The smell of processing crabmeat was nauseatingly heavy in the oppressive air as they swung by the cannery factories to the spotlessly clean marina. She went forward to ready the lines as he edged the boat into the slip designated by the harbor master.

She found herself scanning the marina, unconsciously looking for a man with a telltale slope to one shoulder. There was no sign of him and she was surprised at how taut she was holding herself in apprehensive expectancy. Certainly that man would have dropped whatever plans he harbored now that he knew they were alerted to him.

She went below to put on a loose shift and gather her handbag. She sighed at the blond ringlets framing her face, and brushed hard to get a more sophisticated flip.

They were waiting for her, having changed to shorts and loose cotton shirts.

As they started down the long dock, she saw a man move in the shadow of the building. Her muscles tensed, then relaxed when she saw his square shoulders. Really! She was carrying that incident too far!

She glanced again at the man. He pulled a cigarette out of a package, pausing to light it. He must have used the last match because he laid the matchbook on a nearby window ledge.

She frowned, certain that she had seen him before. Then she knew. She had caught a glimpse of his profile in the office at the marina this morning. What was he doing here?

She sucked in her breath as her eyes widened. Now she remembered where she had first seen him. He was the man she had observed in the reflection of the store window at St. Michaels! He had asked Craig for a match and had walked off with the book of matches. The hairs on her arms prickled in alarm.

He must be following them also! But Craig had been closeted with him for half an hour, so he was no stranger to him. Again she heard the angry voice before he opened the door, and his denial that anything was amiss when she questioned him.

She glanced up at the man striding beside her. His face was granite hard. Grim lines deepened the creases about his tight lips. Had he seen him? He was not looking in that direction now. She turned back to examine the stranger again as they stepped off the dock, but he was gone.

They walked toward the building. Craig paused, looking back to the *Fly Away*. It was a natural gesture of a man checking his boat. But his hand rested on that windowsill, and she knew with a foregone conclusion that before they moved on, the matchbook would not be on the sill when he removed his hand.

She couldn't believe it. What sort of intrigue was he involved in? Her mind raced, trying to make order out of her confused thoughts.

They entered the office, followed by the harbor master. He was mopping his beet red face with a damp handkerchief.

"It's a killer, all right," he observed needlessly. "We've already beaten yesterday's record. Hope the storm comes soon to give us some relief! These stationary fronts sure build up some nasty weather conditions."

Craig filled out the form and was offered a key to the showers.

"We're looking for rooms with air conditioning for the night," he said. "If we can sleep comfortably, we can face tomorrow if it is still like this. But if we're not successful, we'll be back and use this key. Could you recommend a decent place?"

The man named several. "You might not have much luck," he warned. "I hear that the locals who don't have air conditioning in their homes are crowding into them to escape this blasted heat wave. But there's the pay phones out there." He pointed to a bank of phones. "Save yourself the expense of a taxi running around for you and the missus."

Lee stiffened, then turned her back at the sardonic glint in Craig's eyes.

"Did you hear the latest?" The man plainly loved to talk. "I've been listening to the marine radio. Seems like two boats are missing. Maybe you've seen them?"

An icy stillness enclosed Craig before he slowly turned to the man. "Two boats? What kind?" The questions came out with controlled precision.

"One's a twenty-eight foot motor boat and the other a thirty-foot sail." He shook his head. "Piracy, that's all it is. At least nobody was on board when they stole them. Not like the one last week. Found one of the bodies floating over by the marsh at Tangier. Nasty business." The man plainly relished the telling.

"They say they're used to run dope from the freighters that come in here at night. Wouldn't be surprised. But why a sailboat? Not very fast, are they? Been thinking though. Might be smart at that. The government men wouldn't be

127

suspicious of a cruising sailboat. There are always hundreds on the Bay. They gunk hole all the time, dropping anchor in our nice coves. Better watch out for that pretty boat of yours, Cap." His eyes twinkled at the far-fetched idea. "It looks like it could move faster than most." He checked the name on the card. "*Fly Away*, eh? Aptly named, I bet."

Biff was excited by the news. This was close to home, not impersonal like television stories.

"Were they stolen from here?" he asked, his eyes round.

"Yep, though not from this marina, thank goodness. Can't keep watch twenty-four hours a day.

"Here comes another boat. Have to assign him a slip. Wish you luck on a room, Captain!" he called as he hurried out with his bullhorn.

"Wait in here where it's cool while I phone," Craig ordered as he reached in his pocket for change. "Not much," he grunted, examining the assortment.

Lee pulled out her change purse and handed it to him. He took it with a nod of thanks and went out into the heat. She watched him through the window as he thumbed through the yellow pages of the phone book. The cast was making the process awkward. She restrained an impulse to help. He was so damn independent, let him struggle!

It was evident he wasn't having much luck. After a half-dozen calls, he returned. His thick brown hair was dark with perspiration.

"Deliver me from telephone booths," he sighed, then answered her unasked question. "No luck. This isn't a resort town and the pickings are slim. It seems our harbor master is right. The locals have taken over for the duration of the heat wave.

"I saw a taxi call box around the side of the building. Suppose I get one to take us to town so we can get the shopping over with. At least it will be cool in the stores."

The harbor master came in after he left. "Forgot to tell your husband that first phone is out of order. Haven't gotten around to putting the sign up as yet. I guess he found one that works."

She froze. That was the telephone Craig had used to put in his calls! He had put on an act, telling a deliberate lie. Didn't he want an air-conditioned room? After all, it was his idea!

She let out her breath. Of course. The harbor master's story had caused him concern. He didn't want to leave his beloved *Fly Away* unattended in case thieves were still on the prowl. She could understand and appreciate that reasoning. He was too embarrassed to tell them of his worry, though embarrassment was not one of the emotions she would have attributed to that cynical, rock hard man. A faint unease persisted, but she brushed it aside when Craig returned.

"A cab will be here in fifteen minutes," he said. "Have you made out a list?"

She nodded, taking out the paper to add another item she had just thought of.

He pulled out the pipe he carried in a belt holder but did not light up. It was even too hot to hold a warm bowl in one's hands. She watched the strong fingers absently move over the bowl, rubbing lovingly as along a woman's neck. She shivered with the memory of their touch. The fingers continued to rub and smooth as on a worry stone.

Her list was not long, composed mostly of perishables. The supermarket was large and filled with people walking slowly down the aisles, prolonging their time in its cool interior.

Craig picked up a fan on display. "Last one," he said. "Perhaps we should take it. We can plug it into shore current. The moving air will make the cockpit more livable. I'm afraid that's where we'll be spending the night. Sorry you came, curly locks?"

Her hand flew to her hair. "I can't make it stay smooth when I'm on the water," she said defensively. "You'll have to ignore the way it looks."

"Who said I objected?" His finger touched a curl. Her blue eyes flew to him, shining at the unexpected softness in his voice.

His hand dropped. If there had been a matching soften-

129

ing in his face, she did not see it. She saw only the mocking quirk of his lips.

Damn the man! He was back teasing her, certain of his power over her, keeping her off balance so he could play on her emotions whenever he desired. He was too astute not to have seen the eager response on her face. She had never been able to keep her emotions from showing. What contempt he must have for her quick capitulation!

Her anger surfaced, a saving cover that had to be her protection from his barbs, the only way she could end this cruise and still be able to hold her head up. After it was over she could collapse in the privacy of her apartment.

She huddled in a corner in the taxi on the way back, seeking to put every microinch between them that was possible.

Supper was a chicken salad followed with a minty sherbet. It was all they wanted. The sky was a burning, brassy furnace as the sun finally sank. Yet darkness offered minimal relief. The moon came out, not the lovely yellow orb of the other night, but a tarnished silver disc, as if it too was damned by the heat. The fan was a thankful help. It could not cool the air, but the movement helped to evaporate the moisture on their bodies.

"If you bring the bottoms to that pajama set that is getting too small for you, I'll cut off the legs," Lee offered the boy. "I daresay that's all you'll want to sleep in tonight."

He brought them up, grateful for the suggestion.

"Are you going to cut off yours, also?" he asked, watching the scissors cut into the fabric.

"No, I have a bikini I'll wear," she answered.

Craig turned his head. "I was wondering if you owned one. How come you don't wear it in the heat of the day?"

She kept cutting, ignoring his question. He would not understand her shyness over displaying that much of her body to his discerning eyes. He would be comparing her slim, boyish figure with those he had possessed, and she did not want to be on the short side of the scale. A vision of Ruth's voluptuous figure came to mind.

Biff saved her from an answer. "I've tried to go without

130

pajamas like Dad, but at school they won't allow it. I'd rather not wear any. I always get twisted up in them."

"That's because you're a restless sleeper." His father's hand came out to rumple his hair. "I never knew anyone who rotated in bed the way you do. You made it hard for me to sleep last night."

"I'm sorry, Dad," he apologized, resting his hand on his father's knee. "The housekeeper always complains how my sheets are pulled out. The bed has to be completely re-made every morning."

Lee's clear blue eyes filled with compassion as she took in his earnest face. The poor child! If he had a loving home, she bet his nights would be more tranquil. A tender smile hovered on her lips.

"Are you finished with your slashing?" Craig's voice lashed out at her.

She jerked at his barely controlled anger. The lights from the dock held her in sharp relief, but his face was unreadable in the shadows.

What had brought on such vehemence? She had only been looking at his son. Carefully, so he wouldn't see her trembling, she put down the finished trousers and scissors. She rose woodenly and went to the bow, sitting silently on the cabin top.

There, in the shadow of the mast, she let the tears come. She stared stonily ahead into the darkness as they rolled down her face, forbidding any sobs from forming to shake her body so that he could not see her agony. The tears rolled off her cheeks, but she did not dare wipe them away. The gesture would give her away. What, oh, what had she done now to inflame his anger? Had he seen her affection for his son and resented it? Surely he wouldn't think of that as competition!

She was fulfilling her job. He could have no complaints over her performance. It must be because of their encounter the night before. Their bodies had not touched, but she had been vibrantly aware of his full, masculine desire for her. He had been playing with her, but he was aroused with the same passion she experienced. They talk about a

131

woman scorned! Was he making her pay because he had to end with that cold shower? Her heart thudded at the memory, knowing that if Biff had not been there nothing would have stopped them.

Restless, she walked to the bow. The black water sat sullenly with a greasy slick highlighted by the sickly moon. How am I going to last the week? she wailed inwardly. I can't take what he's doing to me!

The noise below in the cabin brought her out of her misery. What was he doing there? She brushed angrily at her cheeks, wiping away the signs of her wretchedness.

She came to the cockpit in time to see them struggling with her bulky foam rubber mattress, and she helped pull it out.

"We'll put it on the cabin top for you," Craig said. "We're taking each side of the cockpit."

"All right," she said. "It might even be a little cooler there." She replaced the fitted sheets. There was no thought of more covering.

Biff brought up the pillows from their cabin. "We decided not to bother with sheets," he said, stretching out on his side.

She turned hesitantly to Craig. "Why don't you take my bed? There is more room there. You can't sleep comfortably on this seat." Tomorrow I can fit in the hollows you made, her mind thought treacherously.

His face was bleak in the shadows as he took in her wan face. A smudge was on one cheek showing where the tears had rolled.

"I might take you up on that offer. The captain does have first prerogative, doesn't he?"

She turned sharply away from the unexpected gentleness in his voice. She was too leery of letting down her hard-won defenses. The next whiplash attack could destroy her.

He left the boat to use the phone, this time using a different booth.

He stood on the finger dock alongside the boat when he returned. He looked out over the water for a long time before he spoke.

132

"I called a friend here in town. They were going out but will stop by for a few minutes. I'll talk in their car. I might go with them, but it won't be for long."

She nodded, and he went back down the dock. Since he was wearing only shorts and no top, he couldn't be planning to go to a party.

A shiny car came into the parking area but stopped too far away for her to see the occupants. Craig came out of the shadow of the building and walked over in long strides. He opened the front door on the passenger side and stepped in. Was there only one person there? She could not see the sex.

How handsome he looked, how very male! If he cast those dark brown eyes with their flaming depths to a woman, she would be helpless to resist. Her eyes were abnormally bright as she stared down at her tightly clenched fists. She was one of many.

The car's motor started up. So they were going away! But it only backed to the rear of the parking lot, away from the bright lights by the dock. Her heart thudded sickeningly. She had assumed he had spoken about a male friend. Men do not avoid lights. In her mind's eye she saw his scantily clad body with a woman's hand running across his wide chest. He had been without a woman at least a week. That was a long time for some men.

Why am I torturing myself this way? she cried hopelessly, wringing her hands. But she knew why. He was miserable and self-centered, cynical and impossible to understand. And she loved him.

Biff came up from brushing his teeth and settled onto the narrow bench. "I bet if they put Dad on the case, he would solve it," he said.

"What are you referring to, Biff?" she asked, focusing her attention back to the boy.

"Dad used to be in the secret service when he was in the Air Force," he explained. "I bet he could find out who's stealing the boats."

"I daresay he could," she said solemnly, not showing her amusement over his childish faith. "I bet your father

133

can do anything if he puts his mind to it." Including wrecking her life, she thought.

She adjusted the fan so that he received more breeze.

"You shouldn't do that, Lee," he protested. "Aim it between us and then we'll both get some as it rotates." He, at least, was considerate of others. He must have gotten it from his mother's side of the family, she thought bitterly.

He was soon fast asleep and Lee decided to go below to prepare for the night—anything to keep her eyes from being pulled as if by magnets to the car parked in the shadows. And the two who were in it.

The abbreviated bikini was the same blue as her eyes. She had been shopping with a friend and had been coerced into getting it. She stretched out on the bench and soon found that the covering sheet was intolerable and pushed it off. She turned her head into the pillow to be overcome with the male scent. Biff had brought Craig's pillow. She had forgotten to exchange it with hers. She rose to rectify it, then sank back, burying her face in its depth.

Oh God, oh God, oh God! she moaned as the complete helplessness of her position overwhelmed her. This was no ego trip she was on. This emotion was too earth shattering, too pride rendering.

She raised her head at the grind of the starting motor. Craig stepped out of the car and watched it leave, pausing to light his pipe.

He walked slowly to the dock, his head down in deep thought. He continued past the boat to the end of the dock to lean against a piling while gazing into the black night. She heard the tapping of his pipe as he emptied the burned tobacco, and the boat swayed as he stepped on board.

Looking up from her position, he seemed to reach to the sky. In a surge of panic, she recalled her dream where he climbed higher and higher up the mast until he disappeared from her.

She drew up her legs so that he could step into the cockpit. He sat down in the space, leaning into the breeze from the fan. Her feet rested against his hips, and she had to sit upright to break contact. He turned his dark head, his lips curling slightly.

"I see you meant it when you offered me the choice bunk."

"Of course. The superior male gets preference, especially when he's captain," she said lightly, desperately wishing she could reach for the sheet. His eyes were too intimate over her body. The bikini was the wrong idea.

His eyebrow twitched. "There's still room for the two of us. And softer than these cushions."

"I've had enough bruises," she said, staring defiantly back at him. "I don't want your cast to inflict more."

The bright lights of the marina went out suddenly to be replaced by the occasional low wattage lights that gave just enough illumination for safe traveling during the rest of the night. The tarnished moonlight sharpened the planes of his face, giving him a satanic look. In an effort to fly from his all-knowing eyes, she went toward the cabin.

"Do you want a drink before bed?" Her voice trembled in spite of her effort at control.

He rose next to her, his body brushing hers in the narrow cockpit. He laid a finger across her cheek.

"It's amazing how moonlight can turn someone into a golden goddess one night, and a silver Sybarite the next," he murmured.

Suddenly she had all the taunting she could take. "If you are looking for a Sybarite, you better go back to St. Michaels. Ruth might still be there!" she said bitingly.

An eyebrow rose. "Ah, but you're here!" Strong hands clasped her bare waist, pulling her close.

Her hands flew up against his hard chest, pushing against his pressure. Her fingers tingled, feeling the muscles slide with his breathing.

"We've been through this already," she said coldly, denying her pounding heart. "I am not in the mood for a rerun. I'm sorry I'm the only one available, but if you're desperate, I'm sure you'll find someplace in town that can help you out!"

"Damn you!" he said icily, dropping her hands.

"And damn you," she countered, anger giving her release from her pain. "But I have no intentions of being played with. When I go to a man it will be because I love him. I am not part of your playground in the sky filled with accommodating stewardesses."

He cut her short, his voice deadly with fury. "Stewardesses are no different from any other females in my experience. You are all eager for the same thing. But you wouldn't know. You've tied yourself in a tight Victorian package. There is nothing wrong with sex."

Her voice dripped with acid. "I agree with you. Only in my little Victorian way, sex and love are part of the same package. Something you evidently have forgotten about."

"Damn you, woman!" It came out surprisingly like a cry of pain. He whirled to disappear into his cabin.

She stood there trembling as dry sobs wracked her body. Oh, darling, she moaned silently, come back and take me in your arms!

Not only was her body reacting treacherously now, but her heart and mind were as well.

She sank against her pillow, shivering with a cold the heat could not reach. He was right. Only a bitch could say those horrid words. She did not know what possessed her. Was it fear that if he recognized the depth of her love, he would take advantage of her evaporating defenses? In her battle to control her emotions she had lashed out hatefully, hoping that she could divert his intentions. She had succeeded only too well. She had killed whatever hope there had been for anything warm to develop between them.

She could have passed the incident off with a flippant retort. Instead she had whipped out like a banshee, drawing blood.

Streaks of heat lightning lit the sky, causing sickly yellow flashes to play over their prostrate bodies. They flared all night, playing a taunting game, but offered no surcease from the debilitating heat, no refreshing rain.

*　　*　　*

136

He lowered the binoculars, cursing around the cold pipe in his mouth. The Coast Guard plane had flown overhead an hour ago, but he could not pick up any patroling boats on the radar screen.

His eyes took in the deck. The collection of crates was tied down as camouflage. It looked like any of the hundreds of old rusting freighters plowing the ocean, hanging on by the skin of their teeth against rising costs. They eked out a livelihood under various flags. Only by coming on board could the Coast Guard prove they were carrying contraband. And unless they wanted an international incident, they wouldn't do that without due cause. It was up to him to avoid suspicion.

That plane would have reported him along with the rest of its sightings. That meant he'd have to force the engines to put out more so that they could make up time lost tonight by the unloading. That way, if he was observed the next day, he would have traveled their projected mileage.

He adjusted the radio to the right crystal. The code should come in soon. Half tonight and the other half at the next meeting place. But not until the two boxes with the white powder were delivered would he get his bonus. That was the big money.

The message came in, and he adjusted his course, satisfied that he would reach the rendezvous on time. The small boats would be swarming out like busy worker ants, carrying their load back to their nests.

He drew on his cold pipe. So far, so good.

CHAPTER TEN

The words that had shattered them the night before still hung in the air the next morning. Craig's face was granite hard, and Lee was coldly aloof. They exchanged a bare minimum of words.

The sun was already putting its brand on the landscape, ready to scorch anyone foolhardy enough to expose themselves to its fire. They took the harbor master's offer of a shower. Even the water from the cold tap came out tepid, and the relief was short-lived when they stepped back into the oven.

A dog was lying in the shade of the building, panting weakly. Lee found a can and gave it water. He turned heat-dazed eyes to her before starting to lap gratefully. She turned to see Craig's unreadable eyes on her, his lips in a tight line, and wondered perversely how he was twisting this little humanitarian act.

She could not rouse last night's anger. Her senses were dormant. They had taken too much of a beating in the past few days and were further drained by the oppressive weather. Her body had been battered physically as well as emotionally, and it cried for rest.

"When are we going to Smith Island, Dad?" Biff asked.

"It's a short run. We'll head there after lunch. By that time it will be intolerable here." The three sat limp in the shade of the awning, a Thermos mug of ice cubes in their hands.

"Of course, if you've had enough, Biff, we could leave the boat here and fly back to Annapolis. But we wouldn't have a place to stay. We'd have to go to Grandma's. My apartment is still torn up for the rest of this week."

Lee lifted her head. They evidently had been camping on the boat when she had first come on board, and she had wondered where he lived. She knew so little about this man. They had not exchanged their inner thoughts except for that first glorious day when their first antagonism had melted under the soul-satisfying pull of a good sail.

"Oh, no, Dad. The heat takes some of the fun away, but I don't mind." Biff turned to her to explain. "The insurance company is having Dad's place redecorated. The apartment above had a broken pipe, and when Dad came home from his last trip, everything was ruined."

"I wish I had been so lucky," she said, smiling at him. "It would be nice to have mine finished when I return. I'm afraid I'm not too expert at swinging a paintbrush."

Craig led his son in personal memories, pointedly ignoring her presence. When the rebuff became intolerable, she left the boat. Was this his way of punishing her for last night?

She was too stubborn to apologize for her caustic words, even if they had been spoken in unreasonable anger. She had been unforgivingly abrasive, but she had meant what she said. She could not go to a man if she did not love him. He had taken advantage of what he thought was an infatuation. Fortunately, he did not know it went deeper. She could hold on to her pride.

She went to the marina office, seeking relief in its air conditioned interior. People from other boats were there also, looking for the same solace. After they exhausted the subject of the abnormal weather, they turned to the usual boat talk—where they were from, where they were heading, and places that they had found interesting. Lee always enjoyed this part of boating. The relaxed camaraderie between boat people was special. But today she felt curiously alien, unable to contribute to the conversation even though they spoke of places she loved.

He's even taken this bit of enjoyment from me, she thought bitterly. Oh, Lord, why did I ever weaken and come on this cruise? I knew from the beginning how he felt about women.

She recalled his emphatic words that first day in Bill's office. "No women!" he had said in that arrogant voice. She should have listened closer to what he was inferring. Male chauvinist, had been her reaction. Male seducer, would have been more accurate.

"It's pretty frightening, don't you think?" The question brought her forcibly back from her unhappy musings.

"I'm sorry. I didn't hear what you were saying," she apologized.

The man sitting by her gave her a quizzical glance. "We're talking about the number of boats that have been stolen lately in this area. There are so many identical boats cruising the Bay now that they're hard to trace, especially if they paint over the names and stay away from the busy marinas."

"I'd think they'd be safer in the busy ones," Lee commented. "They have so much boat traffic that no one has time to notice them. It's the smaller ones where the dock men have more time to observe where they'd be more likely to be caught."

"You have something there," he admitted. "Sort of can't see the trees for the forest. Never thought of it that way."

The talk now turned to the dope smuggling that was so prevalent.

"I still say the Coast Guard is a stepson of the government," the harbor master said, mopping his florid face. "They're swamped with all this extra work, and their budget is less than what the army gets for public relations! They have a tremendous job aside from the smuggling going on now. How can they patrol all our shoreline? You know how easy it is to disappear into one of our creeks!"

They nodded in agreement. That was part of the lure of the Chesapeake.

"They got an old freighter a couple of months ago, but it was almost empty. They pick up the stuff in Mexico or South America and creep in here at night to unload."

"I should imagine it would be difficult to unload at a dock without someone seeing them," a woman protested. "Those bundles are pretty big to hide."

"They usually slip in the hard stuff that way," he admitted. "It's more compact. But the bales of marijuana are something else. They are bulky and can't be hidden, as you say. What they do is park outside somewhere and get unloaded into little boats during the night. They can scoot in where vans are waiting, and it's over in a few hours."

"Oh, so that's why they're stealing the boats," the woman said. "What do they do with them afterwards?"

"Unfortunately, they frequently scuttle them. Those who are more ambitious might paint them another color to sell."

"I hate to think of them destroying the boats. They were someone's joy," she said sadly.

"The bottom of this Bay is lined with sunken hulls," an old-timer spoke up. "Been happening ever since white man settled here." He was evidently a history buff and went into tales about the British occupation.

"The British tax collectors made no bones about the fact they were the King's men and the colonists better pay up. If they tried to avoid payment in out of the way places, they frequently took the produce and scuttled the boats to teach them a lesson. Money was a scarce commodity, and people on this Eastern Shore were never heard from until they had a harvest to take across the Bay to barter. They were treated as outlanders.

"Then there were the pirates. They came from all countries, ready to bleed the isolated plantations. Books are full of their fear of Indians, but the early planters had to fear their own kind just as much!"

"Thank goodness that's all in the past," a woman breathed fervently. "Our generation is much more civilized. At least things have been peaceful until this terrible drug traffic blossomed."

The old man gave a hoot in derision.

"You're old enough to remember Prohibition. These waters saw a lot of rum-running. Many a night gunshots could be heard, and then we'd find some friend or relative was missing, or a boat needed repairs."

"You should know," the harbor master said slyly.

A twinkle came to the man's eye. "I'll admit to it. Down here it was the only way to make a decent buck. I managed to salvage an abandoned boat with a liberty engine which was plenty fast in those days. I got pretty good at recognizing landmarks by starlight."

"I don't believe you!" the woman said reproachfully. This benign, white-haired man with his cherubic face could never have been a rum-runner!

The man's eyes became bleak with memories. "You better believe it. I had a dying wife and a passel of kids. There was no other way I could pay the bills. It didn't pay to spend back-breaking hours crabbing, then get next to nothing for all your work. The market was dead."

"Is that why people get involved now?" she asked innocently.

"There may be an occasional one driven to it just like in my time, but we were in the Depression then. Now there is work available if they are willing to tackle it." His voice became disdainful. "I'm afraid they're mostly in for the fast buck and the excitement. It sure can give that with the law breathing down your neck! They're much better equipped than in my time."

Lee had heard these philosophies often, and her attention wandered. Then, seeing what time it was, she headed back to the *Fly Away* to make lunch. Craig had said they'd be taking off afterward.

They settled for a sandwich and iced tea. Biff, of course, had to have his chocolate ice cream. The boy was sending worried glances between the two. He was a sensitive child and was aware of the friction between the elders. Lee hoped he wasn't putting the blame on her shoulders, although it was partly her fault, she had to admit bitterly, for reacting against his father who hoped to turn her into a passing plaything.

They headed out to the glassy sea. Dark glasses were back on, a necessity as the molten sun glared back at them from the hazy sky and bounced off the greasy-slick water. Their insulated cups were filled with ice cubes. They were existing on them. Lee discovered the cooling effect from rubbing a cube on the inside of her wrist and the back of her neck.

The open skiffs of the crabbers putted slowly by. Long vee's from their wake trailed behind them on the ominously quiet water. The bronzed men worked stoically at their task, scooping the bounty from the waters. It was a hard, but proud life they led. Prices for their catch were better now, and they made a good living. Unfortunately, their sons were deserting the old ways to escape to the mainland and less demanding jobs.

They picked up the marker and started the long trek through Big Thorofare leading to Ewell. The crooked canal was maintained as a pass through the marshy island. Every patch of ground high enough to support a town was built upon.

Wired holding pens came into view where they kept the crabs. Small huts were poised on the narrow walkways. Someone had to watch. When the crabs shed their shells as they outgrew them, they were completely vulnerable to their carnivorous relatives and had to be quickly scooped out. Soft-shell crabs were a luxury item featured in many restaurants and brought premium prices.

The tall reeds were motionless as they ghosted by, the motor sounding queerly muffled by the oppressive heat. They finally inched into the harbor at the sturdy dock.

"I remember when we first came here we had to snake through rotten pilings," Lee said as they tied the boat. "We had been warned not to leave the boat unattended. The natives were living below poverty level and were desperate enough to strip a boat."

Biff looked around apprehensively, ready to protect his beloved *Fly Away*.

"Don't worry, son, that's in the past," his father reassured him. They looked at the houses, neat under coats of paint.

"A lot different, isn't it?" They were the first words he had spoken to Lee that day.

"Yes. The crab industry has prospered," she said, inordinately happy at the sign of a truce. "Still, it loses something. It isn't as picturesque. I wonder if there are any old-timers that still speak Elizabethan English."

She told Biff some of the history of Smith and Tangier, the sister islands to the south. They were reported to have been originally settled by English sailors jumping ship in colonial times. The isolation of the islands had created fiercely independent people. Their language had remained quaintly Old English even into the early twentieth century. Their contact with the mainland, which was also sparsely populated at that time, was minimal. Bare essentials were exchanged for the crabs and oysters they harvested from the sea.

One unhappy by-product of the resulting intermarriage was that the men frequently died of heart trouble in their forties. There were many widows as a result.

Their lives had changed drastically since the advent of radio, then television, plus the law that made the children attend school on the mainland.

The three were content to lie back with their cool drinks and Biff opted for the cabin top with his ever-present book. The town lay quivering under the sun. No one dared the narrow streets. Craig plugged in the fan and its faint oscillating breeze was welcome. The only thing to do was to slide under the heat and rest. Lee felt beads of perspiration form. Small rivulets ran down her body whenever she shifted position.

She woke up to see Craig leaning over her. He was fastening a beach towel on the awning, extending its shade.

His gaze was cool into her startled eyes. "The sun is shifting and creeping in on you," he said.

She pushed at her damp hair, now curling into tight

locks. "What time is it?" she murmured, sitting up to remove herself from possible contact.

"Five-thirty," he answered. "We managed to doze away the rest of the afternoon, and the worst of the heat. Shall we stretch our legs and see what the metropolis has to offer?" A fitful breeze was stirring, making it possible to move.

She smiled at his derision. The tiny town could be covered in half an hour. She reached for another towel and gently wiped the perspiration from the still sleeping boy. Her face softened at the motherly chore. He opened sleepy eyes and smiled at her. Without thinking, she bent to kiss the still childish cheek. He did not pull away as she feared. Still wrapped in sleep, he raised a hand to touch her face. Then, fully awake, he rolled over, embarrassed, all boy. The tender moment evaporated.

She caught the closed look on his father's face, the muscle twitch along his jaw.

Heavens! Was he disapproving of the episode? Granted, she had no right to bestow affection on his son, but did he resent that little spontaneous exchange? He had no cause for jealousy. Biff, for one unguarded moment, had been a little boy remembering a lost mother's love. He could not default her for offering him that.

As they walked around the limits of the town, Craig's mood unexpectantly lightened, and he explained some lore of the island to his son.

"It isn't much of a place, is it, Dad?" Biff said, disappointed by the smallness of everything.

"I guess not to your eyes," he admitted. "But it has an interesting history. We'll only visit this town. Rhodes Point and Tylerton are further in the marsh, and I'm afraid killingly hot under this weather inversion. The local mosquitoes are famous for sucking you dry. I'm surprised they're not attacking us. They must have a better mosquito control than the last time I was here."

"They just have more sense than we do," Lee said drily. "Only fools and Englishmen go out in weather like this. I daresay they are hiding in some refuge waiting to charge us again after this heat goes. Then beware! They'll make up for lost time!"

They stopped at a Methodist church and read the war memorial plaque before it.

"They must have wiped out the Evans family!" Biff said with alarm, seeing they made up fifty percent of the names listed.

"No," his father corrected. "Half of the islanders carry that name. At least they did at one time."

They stopped at the outskirts, overlooking the swampy land. The tide was up and water glinted through the reeds which did their best to hide discarded household goods and ribs of old boats. It all looked so forlorn. What kept the inhabitants attached to the desolate island?

A white heron rose, and beat its wings languidly, arcing toward a far corner to investigate further. The primitive beauty caught at Lee, and she had a glimmer of what attracted the natives. Each person held a different picture of what home was, each one dear and special.

She sighed, thinking of her small apartment, feeling its loneliness. A coat of paint and those new colorful curtains will brighten it, she thought fiercely.

They turned back, exchanging a light bantering which did much to soothe Lee's battered soul. To passersby, they were a happy family, enjoying their stroll. They zigzagged across the extremely narrow streets, making their way from one tree to the next, seeking its offering of shade.

"If we steered a boat this way, we'd be accused of traveling a most erratic course!" Lee observed as they traversed the street again.

"It's a case of survival," Craig said with a smile. "It will be a relief to get back on the *Fly Away* and remove this shirt. Even with the tails hanging out it is too much." The loose cotton shirt clung damply to his chest and back.

They walked through the town, envious of the air conditioners whirring in the windows. They bought the last scoops of ice cream in the small general store.

"Can't keep it in stock with this heat," the storekeeper

146

apologized. "Everyone is living on it. The ferry should be in soon with more. Stop by after supper for dessert."

"Will you have chocolate?" Biff asked anxiously.

"It's on order, but I don't always get what I want."

"We still have some on the boat," Lee reassured him.

They worked slowly on the cones, enjoying the cooled air in the store, deliberately delaying the time when they had to meet the hot air waiting outside.

They gulped when the heat attacked them as they stepped out. As they neared the dock, Craig's attitude again changed. The light conversation stopped and the laughing glints in his eyes disappeared. By the time they stepped on the boat, he had retreated into a cold shell, not even responding to his son's attempt to reach him. It was as if something connected with the lovely *Fly Away* weighed on his soul.

Puzzled by the change, Lee went to her cabin to remove the cotton shift she had put on for the walk. It had been cooler than shorts. Now she put on her bikini. She had overcome her initial shyness. He had seen her in it, and she had survived. The heat made the search for comfort imperative.

His eyes were heavy and brooding as they flicked over her when she emerged, carrying the necessary mugs of ice cubes.

"If you wear your nightclothes now, what will you have left when you go to bed? I can hardly wait." There was a sardonic twist to his mouth before he turned to watch the late crabbers come in.

She was thankful his face was averted as the warm flush colored her cheeks. To wear less was . . . nothing.

The dock master came over to offer homemade crab cakes.

"My wife makes them daily, and I keep them on ice," he said.

Since they were in crab country, they couldn't be fresher, and they bought some.

The cakes were delicious. Lee heated them and tossed a salad. It was all they wanted in the pressing heat. Biff ate his chocolate ice cream, then stretched out to read his book as long as the sunlight lasted.

When it sank, the heat lightning again took over, flashing lurid orange streaks as if in fury with the elements. The humidity was so high that the starlight could not penetrate its film. The moon slunk palely along the horizon as if it, too, hadn't the energy to make its usual climb into the sky.

Sensing that Craig was still not in a communicative mood, Lee lay back on the cushions to watch the display in the sky. She willed her mind to go blank so that she wouldn't have to give a name to the restlessness in her.

Craig finally knocked out his pipe, and they again pulled out the mattress. It was impossible to contemplate sleeping below deck.

This time there were no seductive phrases or sensuous innuendos when the dock lights went down. He gave her a curt good night and settled on the cabin top. She had been careful that he had his own pillow this night. The soft whirr of the fan finally lulled her into a fitful sleep.

The heat lightning kept up its display, the thunder a muffled distant rumble that promised it was biding its time as it girded itself for battle.

He brushed away some rust before leaning on the rail. So far, so good. It had gone well last night without a hitch. The hull was half-empty and rode higher. Late tomorrow afternoon he'd be entering the Chesapeake and the rest, plus the two boxes, would be unloaded during the cover of night.

Too bad he couldn't pause to spread some of his money locally. His lips curled in a ribald smile. Nothing like returning some of the money to its source! He was quite certain their interest was deep in any house he'd be visiting.

He gazed ahead into the dark. Heat lightning was slashing the sky to the north. The weatherman was saying they were baking their brains out there in a nasty weather inversion. It didn't bother him as long as the storm didn't

148

break tomorrow night. He preferred quiet waters for unloading. It would not do to have to sit there waiting for the next nightfall. The spotter planes would pick him up. He would have to make believe he was leaving and come in again. It would mean a lot of extra work and a lot of unnecessary confusion.

Still, a storm would give good cover. Unfortunately they were using too many greenhorns in those small boats, a bunch of kids looking for a fast buck yet scared in any emergency. They had no idea how to cope when the sea was rough.

Even last night with the easy swell two boats had almost swamped. Good thing he had an experienced crew. Only ten bales had floated off into the night for the Coast Guard the next day. Maybe some enterprising fisherman would pick them up to make some private income. That would be far better than having the authorities alerted.

He puffed on his pipe until it went out, then turned into the bridge, nodding to the man at the wheel. He pulled out the next chart and spread it on the charting table. He snapped on the gooseneck lamp and leaned over the table to check the course. After flicking a sliver of rust from under his nail, he ran a thick finger up the chart.

Plenty of good water. He had been here before. His finger paused where the Bay hour-glassed in, then backed down to where the string of marshy islands began. Tangier Island. That was the place. The last of the bales would be unloaded there, and he reached for his plotter to lay out the course.

His practiced eye took in the hundreds of coves and small creeks convoluting the shoreline. It was an ideal place with plenty of room for the local boys to hide if necessary. Those Big Boys planned well, made no mistakes. They were better organized than most governments. Their dictatorships were run as feudal holdings where their word was law.

He sucked on the empty pipe, then sent a stream out the window. He laid the cold pipe down before bending to plot the rendezvous. Had to be careful. He would be tak-

149

ing the boat out of the shipping lane to anchor close off Tangier. It shallowed in treacherously when away from the marker buoys. He'd have to keep a running fix on Tangier Sound Light.

CHAPTER ELEVEN

Lee woke once to a sprinkling of rain. The awning kept most of it away and before she could awaken fully the drops had stopped. The lightning went on unabated, searing the sky with ominous sulfuric flashes.

The sky looked forbidding when they reluctantly got up to find the heat still waiting. The crabbers were already heading out to their private areas. The sunrise was a dirty purple red, causing Lee to recite to Biff the old saying sailors believed in the world over:

> Red sky in the morning,
> Sailors take warning.
> Red sky in the night,
> Sailor's delight.

He repeated the old saying several times, giving it a lilting chant.

"Remember that, Biff," she admonished. "I have found that warning to be based on fact. I'm willing to bet this heat wave will break today, and the rest of the cruise will be more fun."

Craig came out of the aft cabin, bringing with him the clean smell of after-shave lotion and soap. He stared morosely at the red sky, then out of the harbor to the canal they had to follow.

"It's a short hop to Tangier. Are you going to attempt it today?" Lee asked. "The weather might break later."

His chest expanded in a sigh. "Yes. We go today, otherwise we'll have to forget it. We're running out of time. We'll leave after lunch like yesterday." His voice held a peculiar quality, as if he were reluctantly resigning himself to a commitment he rebelled against.

He turned and ran a finger over her bruised shoulder.

"It's fading, and you've added a lovely tan to hide what's left," he observed. "And that wound on your back is practically healed. Bill might forgive me after all for returning damaged goods, but I need to know how forgiving a woman you are, Lee," he murmured. His expression was bleak as he searched her face. This morning the lines were deep brackets lining his mouth. There was a tension in him she could not account for.

"None of it was your fault," she answered slowly. Her eyes darkened at the sensation of his finger continuing its caress along her arm. She knew he was not referring to her injuries but could not fathom what his real intent was.

His finger traveled over her chin to pause over her mouth. Her lips pursed involuntarily as in a kiss. A flame burned momentarily in his eyes to be immediately extinguished.

"Better get breakfast before the heat builds up," he said softly. "I'll settle for some juice, coffee, and cold cereal."

She went into the galley, pressing her fingers to her throbbing lips. How could that light brush feel like a shared kiss?

Craig made a complete about face from his pointed neglect of the night before. He soon had Biff chuckling, and while his brow still arched mockingly at her, there was a softness that thrilled her. She responded as a flower to the sun. Her face glowed, and her clear blue eyes sparkled at his gentle teasing.

They were laughing over a witticism when Biff laid his hand affectionately on her arm.

"Oh, Lee, I wish you were my mother! We have so much fun together!" The cry sprung from his soul, a lonely boy dreaming of becoming a family unit again.

Lee blinked hard against the push of tears. She gave him a quick hug, understanding his need even while her cheeks flamed under the father's hooded gaze.

"Your father will find a mother for you one of these days," she said with a smile, not knowing how much her love for the boy was showing. "Then you won't have to go to boarding school anymore. You don't like it there, do you?"

He sighed. "Not really. I'd much rather have a home like other kids." He looked slyly at his father.

"Now see here, son!" he said sternly. "I'm not going to be coerced by sly innuendos. Before buying, a man first has to look carefully over the available merchandise. Things like size, age, and quality, and how one will wear in the long run are all important to consider." A wicked gleam shone in his eye as he glanced at Lee.

"You mean like checking out a car before buying?" The boy was quick on the uptake.

"Exactly. Or a boat, or house, or even a pipe."

"My." Lee's laugh was shaky. "I didn't realize a man made selecting a mate so complicated!"

"And what does a woman look for besides a steady meal ticket?" He gave her his sardonic smile.

She arched an eyebrow at him. "There's that old hackneyed but romantic thing called love."

"Ah, yes! The snare and delusion offered as bait by wily women," he said with faint derision.

"Surely you have participated in that emotion?" she countered, unconsciously bridling at his tone. "It usually is part of marriage. The first one at least."

"True. It's an elevating experience. And I deduce from what's been told, my much-battered first mate, that your marriage was based on it."

"Definitely. But why, if you've had it once, are you avoiding it as part of your list of desirable qualities for the future, Mr. Lowell?"

He shrugged his wide shoulders. "I've heard the words spoken too often and too readily. The repetition dulls their meaning."

She lowered her head at the hint of scorn in his words. She had not intended the conversation to take this serious and personal twist, but she felt impelled to continue.

"Perhaps you've been expecting too much from the wrong women," she murmured. "Or, again, you're becoming too case hardened to recognize the real from the lightly given sentiment."

She wondered fiercely if Ruth had spoken words of love while in his arms. This disturbing man would easily arouse any woman to that powerful emotion if he so desired— even if he didn't. She was a case in point.

"Why the frown, sailor girl? Surely you don't think I believe words spoken in moments of—er—shared experiences? But then, I must admit I'm basically old-fashioned. I believe love is a case of wanting to give, and it is difficult for a mere male to know a woman's mind. Is she giving, or taking?"

She threw her head up at the barb to find that his eyes had not left her face. It was always open as a mirror. He was taunting her over her declaration of the other night and a faint flush heightened her tan. She retreated from his gaze, her lashes hiding her expressive eyes.

She spoke over her thudding heart. "It's sad, isn't it, how when we're young we don't question love. And when we're older and need it even more, we let doubts rob us of an appreciation of that most important emotion."

"An interesting supposition," he said, filling his pipe. "I admit love would sweeten the pot if all the other qualifications were there." His eyes laughed at her over the flame held to the pipe.

She moved to hide her confusion. There were subtle shadings to the conversation that she was not ready to explore. He had freely admitted to affairs with several women, and that was acceptable. He was an extremely virile man, and women would fall all too readily into his arms. No wonder he backed away from deep involvements. Their easy availability would make him blasé about any new woman he came in contact with. No wonder his recognition of her emotional response to him and his calculated sensuous taunt had inflamed her. Experience had made him a past master in handling women.

She turned to the boy, who was trying to follow the conversation. "I believe your father means he's still looking. So keep your fingers crossed that he finds this paragon of womanhood soon." She looked at the man with faint disdain. "Just make certain she will be a good mother to your son. He deserves the best."

"Of course. That is high on my list of priorities." He was openly laughing at her now.

The angry glow left the sky as the sun climbed. Being a seasoned sailor, she kept an anxious watch at the lowering clouds to the west. Lee could not understand why Craig didn't take off while the weather held. It would be a miserable crossing if the storm broke while they were still on the shallow waters of the Sound. And the entrance to Tangier was another narrow channel threading through very shallow waters, tricky to hold in high wind. Surely he was aware of the danger!

But he was captain, and as crew she could not offer her opinion unless he asked for it. Although his mood was benign at present, she would not overstep her position. He was in charge, and she knew her place.

They were content with a crisp salad for lunch. Lee opened potato chips, ever mindful of the salt they were losing.

Craig finally started the motor, and they untied the lines. Immediately, as if on cue, there was a return of the forbidding sternness to his face as they pulled away from the dock. The light reparté of the morning was over. He had again switched to a remote martinet building a wall she could not breach.

His mercurial moods bewildered Lee. Was he unhappy because he now was aware of the threatening storm? But he was an accomplished seaman and could read the

155

weather signs better than she. Still, perhaps she should have warned him of her earlier misgivings.

She wondered at his willingness to expose his beloved *Fly Away* to possible damage, not to mention discomfort to his son. Biff had suffered from seasickness during the first rough sea passage.

"Do you think we'll get there before those black clouds reach us, Dad?" Biff asked, an apprehensive frown ruffling his forehead. Even he could see the danger.

"It makes no difference," Craig answered curtly. "*Fly Away* has weathered the worst the Bay can offer without a mark. It should give us a few thrills. I'm tired of this insipid motoring we've been forced to do the past few days. How are you at battling with the elements, Lee?"

"I've had my share," she murmured. So that was what he wanted. It could be stimulating, to say the least. Then, seeing Biff's face getting pale, she added, "If it gets rough, we'll break out the life jackets. But we have nothing to worry about. Your father is an old sea salt, and we know *Fly Away* can take anything with flying colors."

He smiled nervously at her, willing himself to take courage from her words. They passed the crabbers hurrying back to safe anchorage. They were the recipients of disgusted glares. Lee could read their thoughts: Stupid landlubbers! Can't read obvious signs!

They turned south into the wide expanse of Tangier Sound after clearing the mouth of the canal. The rumbles of thunder came in waves heard over the throb of the motor.

They looked up in surprise. They had been squinting against the hazy glare on the water and had been unaware of what was brewing to the west. That's where the weather came from. As experienced sailors, they should have been alert to the changing pattern.

The low angry line of clouds was more intense, forming a heavy curtain while marching ominously across the Bay, making black threats to challenge their skills. It was a long time since she had seen anything this intimidating.

They came roiling, anxious as children tumbling out of

a school door bent on mischief. The front had held them in abeyance too long. Powerful sources of energy had been seething independently, and now, as the front moved, they were able to mix and collaborate in an awesome fury. The colder air shocked the water-laden, overheated air. Turbulent clouds rose precipitously to formidable heights, the outer shell hiding the boiling cauldron of elements crashing in an independent circulation.

Tiny droplets rose to freeze into hail, which alternately grew larger and then melted as that inner circulation elevated them through hundreds, thousands of feet of atmosphere.

Lightning, blue and yellow, streaked madly, bouncing from one cloud to the next, adding its garish electrical display.

This was nature primeval, denying man's puny attempts to match its holocaustic abilities. Nothing would survive if it was so unfortunate as to be overtaken.

Fortunately it rode above the surface of the earth. What reached down could be terrifying enough.

Lee felt Biff's hand creep into hers. She took in his white face, his eyes wide with mounting apprehension. He looked at her nervously, overawed by the cataclysmic display.

She gave him a smile full of reassurance. At least she hoped that's what it showed. My God, this was going to separate the men from the boys! she groaned inwardly. She glanced at the man at the wheel.

He was examining the building clouds with a clinical eye. His very calmness came as a surprise after watching the violent elements approaching, and helped clear her head. They were committed now; they could not escape its wrath, but they could prepare themselves and the boat to meet what it had to offer.

The composed assessment of the man was all she needed to see. There was no sign of panic, no apprehension as he took in the threatening clouds rapidly filling the sky to the west.

How much time did they have before it hit them—fifteen, thirty minutes? It was hard to gauge its speed.

A rising excitement tripped through her. She had full confidence in *Fly Away*, and the man at the wheel. She knew she could weather anything with him, her trust in his ability complete.

She did not question why he didn't return to safe harbor. If a storm hit while threading that narrow channel back to Ewell, they would be lifted and deposited on the marshy flatlands, and *Fly Away*'s back could be broken. Any knowledgeable seaman would rather face a storm with deeper water around him if he couldn't be tied safely in a port.

The air was still not moving where they were. It sat heavy, hovering over them, pressing down full of heat and humidity.

Breathing became a conscious effort, making them headachy and thick-witted, but she gave a life jacket to the boy, and hauled out the lifeline from the seat locker, snapping one end around the mast. If she had to go forward during the storm, that line fastened around her waist could save her from being swept overboard.

Lee glanced below at the barometer. "It has dropped several points," she informed Craig.

He nodded. "It feels like it. I'll be getting the opportunity to see if you're as good as Bill boasted."

Wordlessly she went forward to check that the hatch covers were secured tight and lock the portholes. She gave the loose lines to Biff to put in a locker, then checked the sails to make certain they were tied down securely. With a critical eye, she looked over the topside to make certain nothing loose could trip hurrying feet.

"Shall we take the dinghy back on board?" she asked. The boat had spent the voyage trailing behind them.

"I don't think it's necessary," he said. "I put a new rope on it and it's not frayed. Just check the knots."

She hauled the boat close alongside and secured it before lowering herself into it to add another knot with the

158

trailing end. She then undid Biff's simple knot and refastened the line to the mother boat.

All sound was muffled in the weaving, moisture-laden waves rising in the air caused by the massive evaporation. They appeared isolated in their heat-shrouded world. Land was not far away, but was too low to be visible in the haze.

Craig stood up by the wheel to peer ahead, then asked for the binoculars. He focused on the water ahead.

"Looks like a boat in trouble," he said. His voice sounded so harsh that Lee turned quickly to look at him. The heat was really hitting him. He seemed to have aged suddenly. His shoulders sagged as if unbearably weary.

She squinted into the glare, finally locating the gray smudge dancing in the misty haze.

Craig did not change course to investigate. It was five minutes before they were close enough to clearly see the outline of the old boat. Two men were huddled over the quiet engine. Not until they were almost abreast did one man stand up to wave both arms in the approved distress call for help.

"They're asking for assistance," Lee said, surprised that he wasn't responding right away.

Craig nodded. Tight muscles were jumping along his jawline. His arm must have been itching again under the cast because he slipped his hand into the sling to scratch. It was a useless reflex action, since no relief could be felt through the rigid plaster.

"I was mentally reviewing the chart to remember if the water was deep enough to get closer," he said.

His eyes were hidden by the sunglasses. She could not understand his seeming reluctance to turn the wheel. Surely, as good a sailor as he would hurry to help another sailor in distress, especially with the promised storm bearing rapidly down upon them.

He finally slowed the motor and started a wide circle around the boat as if not anxious to come closer.

The man stood up, cupping his hands to his mouth to

amplify his words. "We lost the screwdriver overboard. Can we borrow one for a minute?"

Lee hurried below to where the tool box sat and brought up the set.

"What kind?" Craig called.

"Medium-size Phillips," he answered.

Lee selected one, and Craig inched nearer the boat.

It happened with quick precision. One minute she was leaning far out, offering the tool in her hand, and the next an iron hand grabbed her arm, pulling their boat against the *Fly Away* with a thump. The other man leaped up from the engine and threw a rope around a cleat, tying the two together. She heard Biff cry out in alarm as he grabbed at her legs, and she lurched over the water with the pull.

The man pushed her roughly back into the boat and climbed on board, gun in hand. The second man joined him, aiming a rifle at Craig and forcing him back behind the wheel.

Not until then did she recognize him. He still wore a mustache, and his shoulder hung down at a sharp angle.

Biff recognized him also. He gave a bewildered cry. "Why, you're my friend!" he exclaimed before fright covered his face at the sight of the guns.

Lips curled in a mirthless smile. "Never had such good results from one chocolate ice-cream cone. You're a nice friendly boy. Now behave intelligently, and your parents won't get hurt."

A loud crash of thunder interrupted him. He glanced at the black clouds rolling angrily toward them. "You better take your boat and get out of here, Mike," he said to his partner. "That storm is about to hit, but it's moving fast and shouldn't last too long. I'll get rid of the captain here. The little woman can help me sail. I've seen her handle the boat, and she knows what she's doing." His eyes swept coldly over her body exposed in the bikini. "She might even prove an interesting diversion waiting for the freighter tonight."

Craig stood up and the man aimed his rifle at his broad

160

chest. "I can't miss at this distance, Captain. Behave and you'll get a few more minutes breathing time. You're expendable. You're too big and might cause trouble. But your wife here will be more tractable, especially if she wants her son unharmed."

Lee drew the trembling boy to her, holding him close in protecting arms. He had assumed that they were a family vacationing on the water, but this was not the time to correct him.

"There's no need to threaten my—my husband or my child," she said, surprised at how cool her voice came out over the turmoil tearing in her. "I'll do what you want now and—and later, if you leave them alone. You can lock them in the aft cabin where they can't cause any problem to you."

She saw the swift fury in Craig's face as the man gave a coarse laugh. "I usually keep them to help in the loading, but your man is no good to me with one arm. I'm getting rid of him now so I don't have to waste time later. Too bad for you that you owned such a good boat for my purposes. It's faster than the usual sailboat. I'm keeping you and the boy so we look like the usual cruising family if anyone becomes inquisitive."

They were hit by a sharp gust of wind from the approaching storm, causing the boat to heel sharply. Craig made a lunge at the man while he staggered to remain upright. The distance was too great. The man regained his balance enough to raise the butt of his rifle and crash it over Craig's head. He collapsed with a groan.

Biff let out a scream and dived to his father. Tears streamed down his face as he pulled at the inert form.

"Help me throw him overboard before you go, Mike," the man ordered, and Biff rose to battle with him. The hand raised and cracked him across the face, sending the boy spinning backward. Lee gathered the stunned child in her arms and crushed his struggling form. They watched in horror as they lifted Craig's unconscious body and swung him over the side.

The splash as he hit the water was a death knell in Lee's

161

heart. She was too shocked to cry out as she tried to restrain the hysterical boy from leaping after his father.

The rifle was raised, waiting to send a bullet into the body if it came floating up, but the storm was almost upon them. The boat again rocked as the winds buffeted them, and Mike hurriedly cast off and raced for the mainland in an effort to outrun the storm.

The man turned and dragged Biff roughly to the cabin. He thrust him down the steps and locked the door.

"Get some rain gear for us," he sneered. "Hurry unless you want that beautiful body beaten by the rain. And don't try any funny stuff. The boy's life depends upon how well you obey orders!"

Lee obeyed. She was too deeply in shock to think for herself. Burned in her mind was the sight of the body of the man she loved as he was thrown over the side, and the horrible sound of the splash as he hit the water. He was unconscious, and the cast on his arm would act as an anchor to drag him to the bottom. She felt like Biff. She wanted to jump after him and follow him down to the cool depths. Her arms wanted to hold him close to her through eternity.

Instead, she brought up the slickers and handed one to the man. He was now behind the wheel, pointing the boat into the wind. It was the only way to ride out the storm.

She would welcome the rain beating down on her exposed body. Perhaps its beating would ease her torment, but when the first gust hurled the raindrops like hailstones, she put her arms into the sleeves, then sat dully on the cushion to wait for she knew not what.

The wind howled like a tormented soul as it whipped at the awning, threatening to tear it from the restraining ties until the clouds opened up with a deluge that flattened the material. The boat shivered like a whipped dog as it cowered under the fury of the unleashed elements. The area suffered for too long under the unrelenting heat wave. The sudden introduction of cooler air caused a cataclysmic reaction. The thunder reverberated hard after the slashing lightning. There was nothing to do but ride out the storm.

The intense fury lasted a half-hour. As the crashing bolts of lightning moved eastward, the boat lifted its head as if to shake itself and say, well, that wasn't too bad.

The temperature plummeted fifteen degrees and, while the awning helped protect them a little, the swirling winds had sent the rain over them. Lee shivered at the wet plastic clinging to her bikini-clad body.

"Go put on a sweater," the man ordered brusquely.

She was surprised at this show of consideration and hurried down. She whipped off the bathing suit and slipped into slacks and an enveloping sweater. Perhaps if her body were covered, he would forget his threats.

She huddled in a corner furthest from the man, too numb from the swift change of events to feel the depth of her grief. That would come later, she knew.

"What's your name?" the man said, peering into the rain that was finally showing signs of slacking.

"Lee," she replied. She was about to give her full name but hesitated. He had assumed that they were married and if he knew Craig's name, would wonder. Not that it would make any difference now. After he finished his mission, both she and Biff would be expendable and would follow Craig. They had seen faces and would be witnesses, and the men knew they were living on borrowed time.

"You can call me Joe," he said. "No use calling 'hey you' when I want something. Right now I could use a hot cup of coffee. Make it two. Two sugars and light with milk for mine. And, Lee, don't put anything in it. You're going to be my taster first." His smile did not touch his hard, black eyes.

The coffee had no flavor to Lee, but its heat spread a little warmth into the frozen ache inside her. When they were finished, he ordered her to take down the awning. There was a surprising blue streak in the western sky, and the rain would soon be over. He would want the sails raised shortly.

The awning was heavy with rain. A small pond had formed, filling the sagging material. She managed to push up the center, dumping out its wet load. After rolling it

163

up, she tied it neatly on the cabin top. Oh, Craig, you loved this boat so much, her heart cried, not realizing that was why she worked so lovingly.

He told her to unroll the jib. *Fly Away* was meant to sail. She sulked when under motor and had been insulted by its use the past few days. She now lifted her head, begging for more sail, and as soon as the rain lessened, the man obliged by heading into the wind to make it easier for her to raise the large mainsail.

He handled the wheel with a satisfied grunt. "Always wanted a boat like this. Maybe I'll keep her. Paint her hull a different color and take her to Florida. Not a bad idea." His eye roved over Lee. "Too bad I can't trust you. You'd make a good first mate. Above and below deck."

She quailed under his leer. "Why did you have to choose this boat?" she asked, searching for a subject away from her.

His shoulders twitched in a shrug. "The order came in, and I happened to be in *Gratitude* when you arrived. I could see she was a beauty and had more speed than the usual sailboat. I'm an old sailor from way back and was taken by her. Then, when your son said you were heading to Tangier, I decided she was for me. I'd let you take it down until I needed her. All I did was follow you to check if you'd arrive on time for the takeover. You timed it perfectly." His sardonic grin chilled her. "Too bad your husband had to act the hero, but I really didn't need him to load up on this trip. The Big Boys want me to take on the special stuff, and that doesn't take up much room."

She knew he was talking because he had no fear she would repeat his tale. When he delivered, she would be no more.

The boat went happily along, gliding with the pull of full sails. Still, she did not fly as under Craig's hands. She was holding back, unable to make up her mind if she should show off for this stranger at the helm.

Lee was conscious of the slight reluctance of the boat, as if a sea anchor were out. She wondered if the poor dinghy being pulled behind was full of rain water, causing the drag, but decided against checking. If the boat did not make the meeting, perhaps they might be saved for another try. It was a slight hope to cling to.

The sun was sliding down to the west at a faster rate. He must also have realized too much time had been wasted while waiting out the storm, and he reached to turn on the key to engage the motor.

Lee pointed to the dial showing their speed. "You won't get anymore out of her with the motor. Her hull speed is six knots, and she's at it already." She did not say how Craig could cajole extra speed out of her.

"I'm getting hungry," he said. "Fix me something good. No use saving the best for later, is there?"

No use at all, she thought bitterly. If there had been something to put in the food, she would have done it. At least then he would pay for the horror of Craig's death. There was little hope for Biff and herself.

She opened the drawer and took out a small paring knife. It wasn't much, but she could hide it in a pocket in her slacks. It might give her a momentary edge if he carried out his threat on her person. Would she have the courage to use it? She thought of the sound of the splash when Craig's body hit the water, and felt a deadly resolve for revenge.

She took out a steak and pan-fried it quickly while heating canned vegetables. This was not one of her gourmet attempts to please Craig. She brought up the tray and asked if she could also feed Biff.

"If you wish," he said indifferently. "Just don't go into the cabin with him. He can come to the door."

She unlocked the cabin and called to the boy. He was not on his bunk but had crawled to his father's bed. A jacket of Craig's was crushed in his arms. He turned a pale, tear-stained face to her, and her heart contracted.

"Here's something to eat, Biff," she said gently. "I gave you an extra serving of chocolate ice cream."

He smiled wanly, shaking his head at the food. Like her, he could not bear the thought of eating. She mixed the ice cream in the glass of milk and urged him to drink the concoction.

She then sat in her corner, waiting for Joe to finish eating. She thought of rushing him with the knife, but his hand was never far from the rifle laying next to him. The sound of a motor came through the numb wall that cushioned her. She looked up with hope, but it was only two crabbers coming out now that the storm was over. They must be from Tangier. The only difference from the boats seen at Smith was that these contained several men instead of the solitary crew.

She sank back in dejection, but Joe searched the boats that were increasing in number. Then, apparently satisfied, he leaned back to enjoy the sail.

"You better get your son up, Lee," he muttered when several of the boats came close by. He glowered at them with annoyance as they bent to their tasks. "We are the happy family, aren't we?" he sneered. "Have to look the part."

Biff emerged reluctantly at her call. He sat close to her, glowering at the man belligerently, but childishly content to sit within Lee's protecting arms.

"What time are you meeting this—er—boat?" she asked.

"When it gets dark," he replied. He answered her questions with no qualms. "See that freighter out there?"

She squinted into the setting sun and made out the faint outline of the boat. "Up from South America?" she asked. There was no need to ask. The usual source was from there or Mexico.

"Yeh. You'll see a lot of action when the boats come for their loads after dark." He worked his shoulder that sagged as if it pained him. "I'm finally in with the big stuff and that means big bonuses. That's why I was careful about what boat to pick when I decided on yours. No slip-ups are allowed. You get one chance with these fellows. If you keep your nose clean and everything works out all right, they remember you when bigger things come up." He looked over the boat with satisfaction, as if already the owner. He then concentrated on her, making her skin crawl under his thinly disguised, possessive stare.

"Perhaps you better tell your son to go below," he murmured. "We have an hour or so to kill before we are to meet."

"No!" The protest came out strangled in fear.

He popped a harsh laugh. "Suit yourself. You want him as an onlooker? Then he won't have to crawl in a corner with a book to find out the facts of life," he said, reaching for a rope to tie down the wheel.

Her eyes grew large with terror.

"Get back in your cabin!" he spat out at the boy. Biff jumped up and ran to obey, sobs heaving his chest.

She looked around helplessly. No, not that! Her hand dropped to her pocket, but the feel of the small knife gave her scant comfort.

For the first time Lee knew the full demoralizing power of fear. It was a physical force, giving off a burning acid smell, a dry metallic taste in her mouth.

A cabin cruiser came near. Two men waved as they tested their fishing lines. She breathed a sigh of relief, praying they would remain close. They adjusted their lines as they paralleled them on the port side.

Joe lowered black brows in a frown as he glared suspiciously at them. He swung to watch a crabber angling toward them from the other side. It was late for them to be fishing, but the storm had delayed their work.

She looked around. There were an abnormal number of boats out this late. This area was away from the heavy population, and she giggled hysterically.

"It looks like your assistants are all out to meet the same freighter. It's like Broadway and 42nd Street!"

He examined each boat, then snorted in disgust as he accepted her diagnosis. "Damn fools are too eager. Hell, if a spotter plane decides to fly over here, they'll get suspicious." He glanced apprehensively at the sky, then growled. "Don't they have sense? If they louse this up for me . . . !" His face shriveled into a mask of frustration.

He had planned carefully and had been so sure of the bonus that he had already spent against it.

Lee closed her eyes, weak with relief. He would have to stay alert in order not to run into the circling boats. She was safe for the moment.

The light drizzle that had persisted finally stopped, and the sun sank in a clear blaze of glory. Tomorrow would be a beautiful day, and everyone would rejoice at the end of the heat wave. She shivered in her corner. Would she be there to see it? At that moment she did not care. The pain at the sudden end of that tall, dynamic man stabbed her. She would never feel his kiss, or those strong arms around her in love. She ached for what might have been. With dry, burning eyes she stared out at the encroaching darkness.

The cabin cruiser weaved back and forth as it trolled, never far from them. Their running lights came on as the sun gave a last burst of color. She smiled bitterly at the ironic situation. The boats that were going to transport the illegal marijuana to waiting vans were her salvation. The owners would have laughed at the idea that they were acting as chaperones, protecting her from the morals of the dark, merciless man at the wheel. He was forced to stay there to steer a careful course.

She wondered what time he would make the rendezvous. After he picked up his parcels, he would take off to his private dockage. Also, all the boats would scatter, taking their protective presence with them. Would he still have designs on her? Hopefully he would be in too much of a hurry to be interested in carrying out his threat. Or was he the type that would be carried away with euphoria at his success and decide that she would give him release? The revulsion shook her, but she did not panic. Would there be an opportunity to barter for Biff's life?

The small, thin boy had become very dear to her. He was all that remained of his father. To save him, she would do what the man wanted, promising anything if it would spare him.

She would have to wait until he made his contact with the freighter. Could she then play the role of a siren?

He was muttering angrily as he huddled over the wheel. He did not like all those boats. There were at least six now.

"They're supposed to come out at different times," he fumed. "I'll have to get my stuff and get the hell out of here."

The bleak outline of the rusty freighter loomed ahead, a barely discernible red and white light hung low at the stern, no doubt as a signal. He ordered her to lower the sails and turned on the motor for easier handling.

He picked up his rifle and told her to get the boy into the cockpit. He ordered Biff to sit by his side and aimed the gun at his head.

"I'm going to pull alongside by that ladder," he said coldly. "A man will have two packages. I don't know if he'll turn them over to you or not. Handle them with care. If you drop one overboard, you know what will happen to your son. Do I make myself perfectly clear?"

"Yes," she whispered. He was not a person to cross. The cockpit was filled with his evil intent. Biff sat frozen in terror. She started to go to console him.

"Don't get any closer." The threat in his voice effectively halted her, and she backed away on trembling legs.

The freighter rose ominously over them in the dark. The moon was on the wane and not out as yet, but the stars gave a surprising amount of light. Joe maneuvered the *Fly Away* toward the rusted hull, and Lee hurried to lower bumpers to protect the sides. Even now she couldn't let the boat Craig loved so much be damaged. The sea still rolled from the storm. The oppressive heat no longer pushed it into an oily mirror.

Joe pulled a pocket flash from his shirt and sent a yellow beam of light in a flashing code to the bridge high above. Beside them, the black form squatted like a huge spider, obliterating most of the sky. The diesel pumped like a throbbing heartbeat deep in its bowels. Ahead there were splashes of water as the bilge pumps worked con-

169

stantly, as if sending out its life blood in streams of dirty water.

Lee heard the slapping of the rope ladder and made out the dark shape of a man hurrying down. It was tricky keeping the boat close, and she was kept busy fending them off. It could easily smash against the side in the heaving sea.

The man leaped nimbly onto the boat. There was no package in his hand. Joe rose behind the wheel, swinging the gun at the new passenger.

"Don't get nervous," the man growled. "How did you think I'd get down here carrying anything?" He pointed above him.

A rope was being lowered. He reached for it and pulled it into the cockpit, then opened the attached net and extracted two bundles.

"This what you're all hot over?" His swarthy face split into a mirthless grin. His look was evil as the glow from the red light from the binnacle highlighted his face. "They said nothing about money so I guess you've made other arrangements, but this you have to sign for." He pulled a square of paper from his hip pocket.

Joe hastily signed and circled the boat back against the hull. The man caught the ladder and quickly disappeared up the side.

He took the two bundles and pushed them in the seat beside him, placing a protection of cushions over them. Then with a sigh of accomplishment, he gunned the motor to put distance between him and the circling boats.

"Put up the sails," he ordered. His voice was jubilant now that contact had been made and success was his. There would be a long celebration after the waiting car paid him off. He had felt the weight of those packages. It was a big shipment, and they had trusted him. His eyes glinted with satisfaction.

He squinted into the night as he weighed his daring plan. Should he ask for more money? He was bringing in more than they had indicated. Surely he should get a percentage. Reluctantly he pushed such errant thoughts away.

One shot and someone would eventually find his body. This was no time to let his avarice take over. If he kept his nose clean, he'd get better assignments, and then who knows?

The rifle was over his knee. Seeing his attention diverted as he concentrated on the boat, Biff inched away. Joe saw the movement immediately.

"Get below, brat," he sneered at the quailing boy. "You've served your purposes for now."

Biff hurried to obey, relieved to escape the menace he represented.

Lee stood by the bow, loathing to return to the cockpit and the man at the wheel. The sails were up and the motor on. He was anxious to get the most out of the boat.

She heard the noise of the helicopter before she saw the black shape against the starry sky. There were no warning blinking lights, and she wondered dully if it, too, was picking up a consignment. She looked back at the receding freighter. The cruiser that had played at fishing was following close behind. They, too, had evidently picked up their load.

Suddenly the sky was illuminated in a bright light as a high-powered beam from the helicopter burned down upon them, outlining the freighter and the surrounding boats in an intense glare. Orders over a bullhorn blared out but they were too far away for her to hear the command. The small boats started scurrying like frightened water bugs.

It happened so quickly that she could only stare in amazement at the tableau silhouetted against the black night.

Her first reaction was intense thankfulness that the unloading was halted and the drugs would not reach a market. Her second was of bitterness. They were too late to save her and Biff.

Joe, after the first startled glance over his shoulder, now leaned forward over the wheel as if urging the boat to its utmost speed. She went to the cockpit. He'd be after her to work the winches to tighten the sails.

The cruiser came abreast, and Joe swung the rifle at

171

them. Ignoring the threatening gun, a man leaned over and called to him.

"We just made it, didn't we? We're lucky this time. Saw you got the big payload."

Joe swore. The transaction had naturally been visible to those close by, and the cruiser had been on their heels.

"If you need speed, come on board and we'll get you out of here in no time," the man continued. "We've got the engines to outdistance anything the Coast Guard has."

Joe's eyes narrowed in thought. He looked back to see the efficiency of the Coast Guard busy in a mopping up operation. They were on the outskirts of the glare and might still be unnoticed. He should make his escape, though he would feel happier on the swifter boat. If they followed him, he would have to dump the stuff overboard, and felt a cold rivulet of sweat run down his back. He wouldn't dare return then. The size of the packages showed this to be an exceptionally large haul. The Big Boys would not take kindly to losing this consignment and chances were that they would not take his explanation for ditching the stuff, thinking he had planned poorly and panicked.

Still, he hesitated over the change of plans. The sailboat had been their idea, and they would be expecting to collect from one. If he turned up in a power boat, they'd fade into the night though they'd contact him later. Did he dare trust these men?

A Coast Guard boat detached itself from the herded boats and started in his direction. There was no time for further thinking. He picked up the two packages and the gun.

He walked to the door of the aft cabin and aimed toward the boy's bunk. The noise rocked Lee as he pulled the trigger. With a scream of horror she jumped at him, knife in hand.

As if viewing a slow-motion film, she saw the rifle swing toward her. The report from the gun became one with the pain that seared through her.

*   *   *

As soon as the white glare of the light illuminated his boat, he knew it was all over. The freighter was too slow to do any maneuvering, and he could see the Coast Guard cutters bearing down on him. One of his friends in a similar circumstance had set everything on fire, but his had been a wooden boat. He could not accomplish much in this rusty hull.

He looked out at the scurrying boats, wondering bitterly who had tipped off the police. The Big Ones had slipped up somewhere. They were not infallible after all. He had received no code that there would be trouble.

His men would be exported, but he would have to face charges. Their promises about protection better be true. He was a good captain, and they would need him in the future. The fact that he was captured was not his fault. The leak was on land. Their bank of lawyers better wrangle a light sentence for him.

He sent out a string of curses. The night before he had played with the idea that it would be diverting if he could sample the women here. Perhaps, when he got out on bail . . .

He put his pipe in his mouth as he waited for the boarding and lit the tobacco with a steady hand.

CHAPTER TWELVE

There were strong arms holding her tight against a hard body, and she vaguely recalled that somewhere she had dreamed of this sensation. It was more comforting than she had imagined, and she snuggled closer into its protection. There was a confusion of voices, and she wished they would go away and leave her to her happiness. She was here at last, into eternity. Where had she heard that expression before? It was too much of an effort to think, and she sighed a name as she drifted into darkness.

There were jumbled impressions of throbbing motors and other arms lifting and carrying her. She tried to respond to the occasional question to reassure them she was all right. But the shock held her inert, and she flowed unresistingly as if on a raft. She had been taken from those special arms, and she would awaken when they returned.

Not until bright lights were aimed at her could she marshal her thoughts. She opened her eyes and knew she was in the Emergency Room of some hospital.

She sat upright and grabbed at the nurse. "Biff! Biff! Is he here?" Her eyes were enormous in her white face. Dear God, let him be alive!

"I don't know about any Biff," the nurse said kindly, gently releasing her clasping fingers.

Lee sank back with a cry. He had succeeded! First Craig, and then Biff.

A doctor came in and parted her hair to look at the wound on her scalp.

"You're a lucky girl," he said, concentrating on cleaning the wound. "I have to cut away some of your lovely hair, but that will grow back. A few sutures will take care of everything."

She submitted stoically to his administrations. Her despair made her immune to any discomfort. Biff was gone, too. The depth of her pain was almost more than she could bear.

She asked the name of the hospital and was surprised to find she was near home. They had transported her back to Annapolis, and she wondered dully if it had been by helicopter, hazily remembering the throbbing sound of motors.

The doctor finished his work and looked closely at her white face. "You'll be all right now except for a headache, I suppose. We have a room waiting upstairs for you. I'm ordering a sedative. You'll be fine after a good night's sleep and better able to answer questions." He turned to the nurse, giving his orders, then went out. The lines at the Emergency Clinic never ended.

The nurse left to fill the order. Lee sat up, and after an initial dizziness, swung her feet on the floor. She didn't want any part of the hospital. She could not face the questions she knew would come. All she wanted was the refuge of her apartment so that she could collapse into her grief, alone in its privacy.

She took a deep breath and went to the corridor. The back doors swung open and an ambulance disgorged a stretcher. The man's face was turning blue and the staff jumped to attention. All other cases had to wait until this emergency was taken care of.

Lee walked out unnoticed, ignored in the face of new crises. A taxi drove up and several people hurried out, anxiety showing in their every movement. She sank gratefully into the vacated seat and gave her address. She had no key or money, but the superintendent should be there,

175

and she had some money stashed away in the apartment.

The super was aghast when he saw her. She mumbled a story to placate him, and he hurried to let her into her rooms. She gave him the money for the taxi, finding it impossible to negotiate much longer. She closed the door on his anxious face, assuring him that sleep was all she needed.

Her head was now throbbing, and she took two aspirin before collapsing on her bed. Would the tears come to give some relief? Why had they pulled her back? She had felt near a welcoming death. She had been so close; she had felt the comfort of Craig's arms, had felt his lips on her face. She had tried to turn her lips to meet his, but had been too weak. Even then she had been denied his kiss.

The tears finally started. There were no sobs, only silent tears that rolled unheeded down her face as she stared bleakly at the ceiling. Mercifully sleep came quickly. She was still suffering from shock.

Bill found her the next day. The telephone had been disconnected for her trip. He had raced over when he heard of the search for her, certain that that was where she would be found. The story filled the airwaves as well as the papers. It was the biggest haul in the Bay's history.

The superintendent confirmed his deduction and let him into the apartment. He knew Bill was her boss, and he was still worried over her appearance last night. He had not as yet connected her to the news story.

Bill looked down at the still form on the bed. She hadn't even taken off her shoes. His big hands were infinitely tender as he removed them and pulled the comforter over her.

She stirred at his touch. "Craig," she murmured, and he winced, catching the hopeless yearning. He frowned as she tossed her head. He pulled up a chair and took her hand in his, rubbing it soothingly as he had done two years before.

He had been a damn fool. When Craig had come with

his request, his old heart had immediately contrived to get these two people he loved together. He knew how right they were for each other. He had hoped that two weeks on the boat would open their eyes. He had not worried about a chaperone. He had respect for their integrity and knew Biff's presence would fill the bill. Besides, they were adults and should set their own limits.

He had evidently succeeded. Her unconscious cry had given her away.

He wondered if she was strong enough to answer the questions the authorities needed. She looked so vulnerable lying there.

Her lids fluttered open, and her hand tightened in his as she recognized her friend.

"How did you get in?" she asked shakily.

"You don't think a locked door would keep me away when you needed me, did you?" His booming voice was lowered to an unaccustomed whisper.

"Oh, Bill," she cried. "They threw Craig overboard and then shot at Biff in his bunk!" Her eyes were black wells of misery in her white face.

He screwed his eyes against the sudden pain in back of them as he cleared his throat. Her agony overwhelmed him.

"Well, yes, so I heard," he said inadequately. Deep emotions always floored him, rendering him inarticulate. "You look pretty peaked, girl. Suppose I make some coffee for you and some toast."

He raised his big hulk from the chair and went to the small kitchen.

Poor Bill, she thought through her aching pain. He loved Craig, also. He can't talk about it either.

She heard the door close. There was little food in the apartment and he must have gone out to get more. She forgot that the phone was disconnected, or that Bill might want to relay messages about her. He returned carrying a bag of groceries, and she soon smelled coffee perking.

Trying to fight the lethargy that wrapped her in a

177

cocoon, she took a quick shower and went to the kitchen as she zipped herself into a robe.

"What are you doing up!" he protested. His bright blue eyes worried over her pale face.

"I can't spend my time lolling in bed," she said shakily. "I still have some vacation time and maybe I'll get some painting done." She looked vaguely at the walls. Work, she knew from bitter experience, was the only possible way to prevent this pain from crashing through her.

He gave a snort of annoyance. "You'll have some breakfast and get back in that bed!" He put the scrambled egg and toast before her and turned to fill a mug from the coffee pot.

She stared in dismay at the food. She could never get it past the lump in her throat. She took a dutiful mouthful, not wanting to further distress her friend.

"I can't, Bill. Oh, I can't!" she finally cried as he watched her push the food around the plate.

"That's all right, girl," he crooned. "Drink the coffee." The poor thing was still in shock. It must have been a hell of an experience. "Want to talk about it?" he asked gently.

She raised eyes that were dark wells of misery. "Not now. Later when I can think straight." Darling Bill. He was her strength again, like the last time.

Cradling the cup in her hands, she sipped the hot liquid, thankful that she could feel the warmth creep through her, melting some of the ice encasing her. He watched her in silence, letting his love show to soothe her.

She lowered the empty cup with a sigh, her face tightened in pain. The words came out reluctantly, but she had to know.

"Biff. Where will they hold the funeral?" she whispered.

Bill's bushy eyebrows shot up in amazement. "Whatever are you talking about, girl? Craig took him home to his mother and put him to bed. Had to get a doctor to sedate him, poor tyke, but he's better today. Why did you run out from the hospital? That poor man was out of his mind when he discovered you were missing this morning."

The mug crashed to the table from nerveless hands. Her eyes blazed with joy. "Craig is alive? And Biff?"

"Of course. Didn't you know? I still don't know the whole story. I called to tell him you were safe but kind of peaked. He wanted to call an ambulance to take you back to the hospital, but I assured him it wasn't necessary. How did you escape? I know how obstinate you can be and told him I'd ride herd on you until he could get here later this afternoon. They've got him tied up giving statements."

Lee shook her head, unable to believe his story. She had been so certain they had both been killed. The incredible news flooded her with blinding joy.

He read her emotions as they played across her open face. He cleared his throat and laid his hand on her head. "You love him, don't you, Lee baby." It was not a question. Her face told all.

"Yes, Bill. More than I thought I was capable of." She could not hold the words back. Stars glowed in her eyes as she finally admitted the fact out loud.

He nodded his head and patted her hand. "Do I congratulate you? He's a lucky fellow to get you," he said gruffly.

A shadow fell across her face, and she lowered her head. The flush of joy receded. "Don't bother, Bill. He's not interested in any entanglement."

His shaggy brows lifted with amusement as he smiled at the lowered head. "Have another cup of coffee. I had to notify the authorities, also, you know. They need your story and will be here within an hour. Everyone thought you were under sedation in the hospital, sleeping it off. When they looked for you this morning, the you-know-what hit the fan. You've given several people heart failure."

She smiled wanly and told how she had slipped out when everyone was concentrating on the new emergency.

He shook his massive head. "Well, we found you. Now take your coffee and get back in bed before they come. I'm staying to see they don't tire you."

179

"There's no room in my little bedroom to sit and talk," she protested. "I'll see them in the living room."

"Well, all right," he conceded. "But you take the sofa and it's feet up for you."

She obeyed meekly. He brought in her pillow and a blanket, ordering her to stretch out.

"I feel like I'm doing the Camille act," she giggled, trying to protest. She leaned back, however, when she saw his stern expression.

Her emotions were in a complete turmoil, making concentrated thought impossible. Craig and Biff were alive! The glory of the knowledge was all she was aware of.

Bill let in the men, pausing first at the door to lay down the ground rules. "She's had a hard time of it." His voice boomed in its customary way. "Don't bother her with unnecessary questions."

The men were properly impressed with his towering hulk and came in to introduce themselves. One was a Captain Johnson sporting the Coast Guard uniform, the other a Mr. Blake in civilian clothes. There was also a young man with a near-unpronounceable name who sat discreetly to one side. He produced a pen and pad to take down her replies.

Mr. Blake took over the interview with a cool, unemotional voice.

"Perhaps the best course is for you to tell us the events as you remember them, and we'll interrupt whenever clarification is needed," he said.

At first she resented his seemingly unfeeling attitude to what was a highly emotional time for her, but she soon realized that she could repeat the terrifying ordeal with less stress as she strove to copy his impassive outlook.

Her eyes became black pools as she relived the horror of the evening before. She attempted to gloss over Joe's threat to her person, but he interrupted her.

"We need the whole story, Mrs. Porter," he said not unkindly.

180

Bill rose in distress. One big hand rumpled his unruly hair while the other was balled into a huge fist.

She told of the man's threat to her that had ended with Craig being thrown overboard, and how later she had secreted the paring knife in her pocket. Then later, when he made the next advance, she had been saved by the boats circling nearby.

The man gave a thin smile. "Mr. Lowell was the cause of that, and I'm happy I listened to him. I wanted to stay further back to avoid alarming him."

Her eyes widened in question, and he nodded his head. "Yes, we were in that cabin cruiser acting as fishermen waiting to make contact."

"But Craig—Mr. Lowell was unconscious when they dropped him overboard! I don't understand."

He sighed and sketched in the background. "We had reliable information when and where this freighter was going to unload. We were especially interested in a large delivery of cocaine that was supposed to be on board, as well as the marijuana. Such an exceptionally big shipment usually brings out the big men, and we're hot on their trail. We even had information that they were thinking of using a sailboat to transport that special cargo.

"Mr. Lowell had been in Intelligence before, and we have used his services at times since then. When he was given this vacation, and knowing he planned to spend it on his sailboat, we put pressure on him to help."

He made a wry face. "It took some urging. He didn't want to expose his son to danger. We told him of our precautions. Having that cast on, it made it easy to fasten a sending beeper that he could activate if and when contact was made. That way he would always be covered."

So that was the gun she had thought was hidden there!

"We almost lost his assistance when we contacted him at Solomon Island. The fact that this man was following you made it imperative that he continue. It seems it wasn't only his son he was concerned about." His gaze flicked over her face.

"It was most unfortunate that they tried to—er—dispose

of him so soon. They usually hold off for a while. Luckily the water revived him, and he managed to hang onto the dinghy as it went by when the storm hit. He had activated the beeper, and we were able to move in under cover of the rain.

"We saw him on the dinghy. Fortunately you did not look behind when he floated free so we could pick him up.

"We had hoped to trail you at a distance to see where he unloaded. We figured a delivery that large would not be handled by underlings." He gave a sigh. "Mr. Lowell can be a very emotional man. He made us close the gap and make that offer. He figured you needed our protection."

"Mr. Lowell loves his son very much," she said coldly. "You are lucky you didn't have to answer to him if that shot hadn't missed."

His eyes flickered over her face again, taking in the wide, clear blue eyes and soft, full lips. He sighed again. He could understand the man's threats to take over the boat and ruin their carefully laid plans.

He rose and thanked her. "I don't believe we'll have to bother you again, Mrs. Porter, except to sign the transcript after checking for errors.

"We stopped this one shipment, but didn't touch the ones we wanted." He looked bleakly out the window. "But there will be other shipments and other opportunities. We have to get lucky sometimes."

They shook hands and left. Bill came storming back after letting them out.

"When I get my hands on that stupid man, he'll wish he had gone down and never been rescued," he raged. "To think he'd cold-bloodedly expose you to all that danger and that unspeakable hijacker!" He was hard put not to turn the air blue with curses at Craig's folly. His huge hands kept clenching as if wishing Craig's neck was in them.

She had to laugh at his righteous wrath. "Bill, you'll be giving yourself a heart attack!" She had to change the subject. "Do you know where Biff's grandmother lives? I

182

would love to call to see how he is doing." Then hopefully she added, "Is Craig staying there, too?"

His bushy brows lowered in a frown as he searched her wistful face. He had learned to love her as the daughter he had never had.

"You can ask him when he comes," he said brusquely, seeing her face light up. "He said he'd be here later this afternoon. Meanwhile I'm making you a bowl of soup and you better eat it," he said threateningly. "Then a nap. I have to get back to the marina and see how Ron is making out."

She submitted meekly to his demand, surprised at how hungry she was now. They were alive, and Craig was coming; her heart sang.

"Do you have a spare key?" he asked. "I don't want to annoy the super again. I'll knock once when I come back, but if you're asleep, I don't want to awaken you. You need the rest, girl." He laid a callused finger on her cheek in a rare show of affection.

She smiled as she gave him the key. The darling! What would she have done without this big teddy bear of a man? Thanking him with a kiss, she let him out with a promise to go right to bed.

She planned to take a short nap, then clean the apartment in preparation for Craig's arrival, but her exhausted body decreed otherwise, and she soon fell into a deep sleep.

She was at the wheel, and *Fly Away* was living up to her name. She laughed with exhultation at the feel of her response under her hand. The wind that filled the sails blew her hair into salty curling ringlets. The bronzed man climbed down the ratlines, and the sun glinted in his dark brown hair as he left the mast. He came to her, his shoulders wide, filling her vision. Her heart pounded with trepidation. The sun was on his back, and she could not see his face. It was imperative that she see his expression because only then she would know if her joy would be complete. Why couldn't she see him more distinctly?

She rubbed her eyes and opened them. She could see a

little clearer and put out a tentative hand. "Craig?" she whispered.

He looked into her sleep-drugged eyes and raised a mocking brow. "Who else? Or do you entertain promiscuously?"

Her eyes flew wide as she slipped from her dream into reality. "How did you get in?" she demanded. Then her cheeks flamed as she pulled the sheet up to her neck. As usual, she had slept without nightclothes.

He handed her the discarded robe. "I'll let you zip yourself in, O Virtuous One, and wait in the living room."

He was silently laughing at her display of modesty, but her joy at seeing him overshadowed everything. She hurriedly slipped into the robe, inordinately pleased that there was a hint of ruffling at the neck and cuffs. It was exceedingly feminine, and he had not seen her in anything but boat clothes.

She pulled a brush gingerly through her hair, wincing against the sharp thrust of pain from the scalp wound. She paused to accent the soft curve of her lips with a pink lipstick. With a dreamy smile, she daubed some perfume behind her ears and in the warmth between her breasts. She was a woman going to meet her man, and she hoped he would recognize her as such.

He stood by the window, his face somber, his eyes hooded. An odd breathless silence extended between them as she walked slowly into the room. Surprisingly, she had forgotten how tall he was.

"Hello, Craig," she said simply. She could move no further. Her clear eyes darkened as they hungrily explored his face. There were still drawn lines by his mouth and shadows blacking his eyes, showing the effect of the days of tension.

It dawned on her why he looked different. His arm was free from the cast.

"Why, you have two arms!" she exclaimed. Then, realizing how absurd that sounded, she gave a laugh. "I mean, you're out of the cast. How does it feel?"

"Empty and light. The doctor prescribed hydrotherapy

for the muscles, but it doesn't seem weak." His eyes did not stray from her face.

Shy under the intensity of his gaze, she dropped her lashes while searching for a subject that would put her feet back on the ground. "I—I guess I'll have some time to paint my apartment after all, now that the cruise has ended. Is your apartment finished?"

"Almost."

"How did you know where I lived?" Her eyes were pulled back to his as if by magnets.

"From Bill."

"Oh." She licked her lips, her mouth suddenly dry. What had that matchmaker told him? "How's Biff?"

"He's well and asking for you. The doctor prescribed rest, but he's already bounced back."

"Is the *Fly Away* safe?"

"Yes. Dale is bringing her back."

"H—How's Dale?"

"Fine. He sends his best." Then, with an impatient gesture, he said, "Are you finished talking about unimportant things?"

A quiver ran through her. "What should we talk about?"

"You . . . me . . . us. As I said, I stopped in to see Bill. He read the riot act to me for exposing you to danger. He then gave me your key."

This time she was able to tear her eyes away, lowering them in embarrassment. Bill couldn't have! He wouldn't give her away!

"I've been thinking about some of those vitriolic words you threw at me the other night," he said.

Her eyes darkened with shame. "You weren't very kind to me either," she reminded him.

"No," he admitted. "I'm ashamed of much of what I said. I was fighting something I had no control over. It was all happening at the wrong time. When I'm backed into a corner, I lash out. You'll have to learn to live with that bad habit of mine."

He came over to her, standing inches away as he had

185

that memorable night in the motel room. He ran a finger lightly along the adhesive on her head. His face became still, his eyes guarded.

"I asked you once if you would be able to forgive me. I had no right to subject you to what happened."

"Oh, Craig!" Her expressive face was his answer, and lights burned in his eyes. His mocking smile seemed somehow tender.

"I also remember an unfinished conversation we had, during which I accused you of being Victorian and that there was nothing wrong with sex. What was your answer?"

Her voice agonized in a whisper. "That I agreed with you. B—But for me, sex and love had to be together."

"If I kissed you now, would you tell me to leave?"

She remembered the frustrated pain of that night, and her eyes became deep pools of misery, beseeching him not to taunt her any longer. He took a deep breath, seeing the unshed tears lying there.

His arms went slowly around her, holding her in their curve. A hand went to her chin, lifting her face. His mouth was cool and tender, smelling of his pipe and shaving lotion.

He lifted his head. Her face was glowing with the wonder of his gentleness. Her hands went to his chest and tingled to his warmth coming through the thin shirting. She swayed against him.

"Oh, my darling!" he groaned, crushing her close, this time to fiercely claim her lips. She clung as in delirium as his mouth worked on hers. They parted eagerly under his searching demand. His heart thundered under her hands as she responded, unleashing every pent-up craving, drowning in his passion.

"Do you know how you've been killing me?" he said huskily. "Darling, can you forgive me for how I spoke and treated you? I wanted you to build up a barrier to what was happening to us. I was going crazy with worry over involving you. I was lost, but I didn't want you hurt again.

186

And then, when I saw how Biff loved you too, it tore me apart.

"I had to steel myself against how you'd hate me after you found out what danger I was exposing you to." He paused, burying his face in her hair.

"Those bastards kept pointing out the small likelihood that the *Fly Away* would be coveted. They assured me that you would be safe, that they wouldn't let anything happen to you." His voice was bitter, recalling what actually did occur.

"I've told those damn government men what they can do with their job. I'm never going to assist them again.

"When we found you missing this morning, I nearly went out of my mind. All I could think of was that for some reason you had been kidnapped by the underworld for revenge."

She felt a shudder go through him and reached up tenderly to run her fingers over the tension lines on his face, conscious of his self-accusing torture.

"Don't, don't, Craig. It's over," she whispered. He had given her a rare look into his inner soul. She had seen the tortured man begging forgiveness, and she had given it willingly. But he was not one to grovel long.

He looked deeply into her eyes. Slowly the lights regrouped in the back of his, and he again became the mocking, assertive man that had stormed into her heart.

His hands cupped her face as he took back her throbbing lips, then rained kisses on her eyes, her cheeks, the pulse pounding in the curve of her neck. She felt a coolness across her shoulders as her robe fell from her and his searching hands caressed her until her body screamed for release. His hands dropped, pulling her hips tight against him, molding her to his muscular body.

His eyes were firebrands burning into her heart. "You're not going to send me away," he whispered against her lips.

She shook her head wordlessly.

"But you said you wouldn't have sex without love."

She nodded, tears glistening on her lashes.

"Then say it, woman, say it!"

"I love you, Craig, I love you!" she cried helplessly.

"And so help me, I love you, my future Mrs. Lowell," he answered, bending his head to meet her waiting lips.

He was a tall, spare figure as he looked over the freighter from the bridge. This one was better than most. He had been its captain once before and knew its idiosyncracies. Each ship responded differently, even if built from the same plans.

He turned to look over his crew as they lowered the bales into the hull. It was hot and dusty work.

One slender figure stepped back, brushing long hair from his face. He pulled out a pale yellow silk handkerchief and folded it into a sweatband to tie around his forehead.

His head came up. Soft, liquid brown eyes met his, hesitated a moment, then dropped. The hands fluttered a minute before he returned to work.

He pulled a twisted cheroot from his pocket and squinted against the flare of the match as he watched the fluid movements of the boy's body. He flicked the match over the side and started forward as his eyes darkened in possessive anticipation. The trip north should prove very interesting.

Once you've tasted joy and passion, do you dare dream of

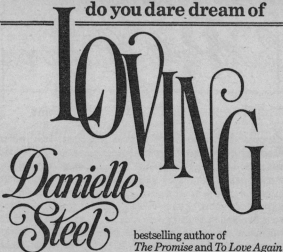

LOVING

Danielle Steel

bestselling author of
The Promise and *To Love Again*

Bettina Daniels lived in a gilded world—pampered, adored, adoring. She had youth, beauty and a glamorous life that circled the globe—everything her father's love, fame and money could buy. Suddenly, Justin Daniels was gone. Bettina stood alone before a mountain of debts and a world of strangers—men who promised her many things, who tempted her with words of love. But Bettina had to live her own life, seize her own dreams and take her own chances. But could she pay the bittersweet price?

A Dell Book ════════════════ $2.75 (14684-4)

At your local bookstore or use this handy coupon for ordering:

Dell BESTSELLERS